THE MISADVENTURES OF MARIA O'MARA

THE MISADVENTURES OF MARIA O'MARA

DEBORAH SKELLY

Riverhead Books
New York

Riverhead Books
Published by The Berkley Publishing Group
A division of Penguin Group (USA) Inc.
375 Hudson Street
New York, New York 10014

Book design by Tiffany Estreicher
Cover design by Megan Wilson
Cover art by Creatas.com

First Riverhead trade paperback edition: June 2004

Library of Congress Cataloging-in-Publication Data

Skelly, Deborah.
The misadventures of Maria O'Mara / Deborah Skelly.—1st Riverhead trade pbk. ed.
p. cm.
ISBN 1-59448-021-4
1. Single women—Fiction. 2. Manhattan (New York, N.Y.)—Fiction.
3. Theatrical agents—Fiction. I. Title

PS3619.K5M57 2004
813'.6—dc22

2004041792

Printed in the United States of America

10 9 8 7 6 5 4 3 2 1

TO MY MOTHER AND BROTHER

THE MISADVENTURES OF MARIA O'MARA

JANUARY 14 I am standing in the half-light of the bathroom at work staring at myself in the mirror. Manhattan takes its toll. I try slapping a healthy glow onto each cheek—hopeless. I am readying myself for the evening ahead. I throw some cold water onto my face and head out the door.

"Maria," stammers one of my filmmaker clients loitering in the lobby. What's she doing here?

"What a surprise," I say with a smile, thinking how much I loathe surprise visits as I wrap her in a warm embrace. "Love the fishnet stockings," I continue, wondering how I can diplomatically have her ejected from the building. And then one of my colleagues appears out of the shadows. Crocodile Boy is in from the coast. He is an aging boy with a shaved head and an insatiable appetite for other people's clients.

"Maria," he cackles as he slaps my back and not so subtly positions himself between my client and me. "How ya doin'?" he asks.

"Fine," I say through gritted teeth.

"I thought I'd take our favorite client out to dinner, and really get to know her. I am such a fan of her work," he continues in obsequious tones. The client smiles. Crocodile Boy smiles. I smile.

I've read that 93 percent of how we communicate with others is nonverbal. I'm optimistic that 93 percent of what my colleague is picking up from me is how much I wish to throttle him. The elevator doors glide open. "Clients first," I say—still with the plastered smile. The client blithely heads into the elevator. "I am going to kill you," I whisper into the back of my colleague's shaved head.

"Relax, I'm a team player," he whispers back.

"So I've heard," I say in hushed tones.

Things at the Agency were getting pretty scary, code for I had a good idea they were not going to renew my contract. In some deep place it was a relief. My immediate boss, The Radical Theatre Agent, whose lack of understanding of mostly everything was his strength, kept telling me, "When they hate you, you know you're winning." But I was becoming wobbly-legged under the pressure. I could get that the clients pin all of their failures on the agent. I could get that when potential buyers (producers, studios, etc.) didn't get what they wanted (because they offered you less money than the other guy, but never mind that small detail) they hated you. I could get that the agents at other agencies were against you. But that all of your colleagues were in competition with you and would just delight in your professional and/or actual demise all the while espousing "team play" and trying to steal your clients just as vigorously as agents from other agencies, that was really starting to undo me.

I rush across the street to the Ziegfeld Theater, late as usual. It is a bitterly cold night. There is commotion and a red carpet adorns Fifty-fourth Street. I flash my invitation, looking around to find my client, one of the three credited screenwriters. It had been a fight to keep his name on the film. He is pissed about the other two writers getting credit. He is clueless that I practically lost a limb making sure his name stayed on the project.

As my eyes pan around the room I see a short, dark-complected man with a navy blue blazer leaning against one of the walls. He is just watching. People in from the coast run in little circles around the theater lobby trying to suck up to anybody who is somebody or has the potential to become somebody. I shake a few hands, do my agent swagger, and furtively look over to see if the dark-haired guy is still there. He is still watching from the periphery, no hype, just calm. I have to meet him. The lobby lights flash. It is time to go into the theater. A senior agent from the California office takes my elbow and ushers me to a seat.

There is a thing about being an agent and never wanting to be left standing alone. It comes from an innate desire never to look superfluous even though we all know we are. And so this big-shot agent holds on to me for dear life, while he projects arrogance and insouciance for anybody who gives a rat's ass and happens to look over in his direction. I try to keep my eyes focused on the dark head, but it gets lost in the sea of heads all here to see what some six-figure-a-month PR firm has dubbed "the most important film of the last ten years."

The cushy seat feels comforting. I wish I could stay in it forever. As the lights go down, I promise myself I will not fall asleep. After all, this is work. There is no sleeping on this friggin' job. Not when an agent who has booked so many gigs he's been made a board member is on your right, and an actress who was nominated for best supporting something just last year is on your left. I hope fate will send the short dark man to me. I hope he is not so sane that he would forgo the afterparty. I feel as if I deserve this. I mean, I have kept my third-rate client's name on this film, and he still has nothing but contempt for me. Haven't I finally earned a chance at happiness?

Circo is bright and glittering. The studio has taken over the restaurant for the night, and it is packed. There is some "secret" little room where it is rumored the real party is taking place. The stars will be there with their managers and agents telling them how great they are, reviewing the brilliance of their performances. Waiters carrying platters with little pizzas keep passing by, but no matter how hard I try I can't get my hand on one. I am starving. I try to look attentive, and like I am working the room, all the while searching for my short dark friend. I try to do it systematically starting at one wall, crossing back and forth with my eyes, but there is not enough stasis. Everybody keeps moving around. And then I see a well-known screenwriter I know I should be trying to sign, and so I try and move in his direction. I am thwarted by a waiter with a tray of champagne. The champagne tonight is quite good. I have downed a couple already. I am captured by some person who wants to talk to me about some really talented person who would be working if only he had proper representation. Christ, I want to shout, I can't sign any more people who are out of work. The agency only gets paid if the clients have jobs. If an agent wastes all of his time doing his job finding people work, he'll starve. The trick is to find people already working, in serious demand, and then just book the deals, *ka-ching*. This is not an altruistic profession, baby. This is dollars and cents, but you can't say that to anybody. It's all got to seem effortless. The agent takes people out to lunch on her expense account and the clients all win Academy Awards. It is fucking beautiful. It's the first snow in Central Park, a pristine Malibu morning. It is success as one finds it in the movies. The minute you sign on at one of the big agencies you are a perpetrator of this myth. Labor is not part of the equation. Labor is for little men below Fiftieth Street selling bird acts.

I find myself standing next to the director of the film. "Wonderful movie," I say. I am sure he will smile and move on. He is handsome, with a dazzling white mane, but with sad blue eyes and red lines in his nose from too much booze.

"What the fuck would you know about it?" he demands. He's drunk. I know this, but his ire still hurts.

"Not much, but if the rest of the schmucks out there like it as much as I do, you've got another hit," I answer back immediately. You must never show the client your fear. He smiles. I know he is pleased with this response.

"I bet you think you're really charming, don't you?" he taunts.

"Not really," I say. I put one of my cards in his pocket and walk away. Tomorrow morning at the staff meeting this will become an important interaction, a planned meeting between myself and this famous South African director, one that shows promise. In the staff meeting notes it will say that Maria O'Mara,

Irish agent to the middle level, has an A-list director in play. Now I will have to plot how to make a real meeting with this talented drunk. How to turn fiction into reality. The reason we are all in show business.

I am tired. I think I feel a sore throat coming on. I wonder if I'll be able to find a cab. It is snowing hard. The short dark man is now relegated to an idea, fodder for a late-night fantasy. He probably did have too much sense to come to this party. I hug the coat check girl, who is married to the pastry chef here at Circo. She has just returned from visiting her family in Italy.

"You look tired, Maria," she comments. "Perhaps I should find you a couple of furs in here. You know—to finance your early retirement."

"Not enough," I say.

"But you gotta start somewhere." She smiles back as she hands me my coat and blows me a kiss.

I head out onto Fifty-fifth Street, not a cab in sight. My plan is to head over to Central Park South and stand in line at one of the hotels as if I am an out-of-town hotel guest who needs a doorman to find me a cab. Several paces ahead of me is, I believe, the short dark man. He is wearing a ridiculous lamb's-wool overcoat. He seems to have a line on a cab. My heart is pounding. How much do I want from God? I make a run for it. The snow-covered sidewalks make it difficult, but I know I must catch him and get him to share the ride, a thing which is just Not Done. But this may be it, my big chance. Next month I will be forty.

I have this theory, the Tacit Agreement theory. In the first few seconds of meeting, the couple's dynamic is established. It may be fate, or how the two individuals interact, but whatever happens, whatever relationship is expressed is a lock. It can take years of circling it to finally admit to it, maybe even a lifetime, but it always goes back to those first few moments.

It feels as if I am gliding as I maneuver my way into him. It startles him. He turns abruptly, preparing to fight off an attack.

"Let's share," I begin. He watches as I step past him into the cab. I can see his expression change as my long coat flies open and a good part of my stocking-clad thigh is exposed. He is no longer frightened. He is hungry. I silently thank God and my mother for long shapely legs.

"Who are you?" he asks in a manner that demonstrates he is up for the game.

"Eighty-first and Central Park West," I reply, trying to seem as if this is all about the business of getting from one place to another, not about spying and tracking. I had a business meeting with an actress once, a notorious stalker. "You know," she'd said, "I don't know what they're talking about. Stalking? What's that? I like to think of it as driving around and hiding in the bushes. I mean, that's what it is," she nonchalantly noted. "What's the big deal?"

It feels good to be going after what I want even if I don't know what that is. His eyes are big and black. He seems to radiate kindness. He is still uneasy about sharing the cab.

"So did you grow up in Manhattan?" I ask.

"Why?" he asks.

"Oh, you did," I say. "Because I didn't, so I think it's okay to share cabs," I explain.

"Oh, I see." He smiles.

The city is silent all of a sudden, the way it gets when enough snow has found its way onto the street. I wish I could stay in the cab with the man with black eyes forever. We head up Central Park West with purpose, the three of us—the cabdriver, the man with black eyes, and me—alone with our thoughts, together in the quiet. It feels safe and titillating at the same time. I have the compulsion to reach over and hold the dark man's hand, but I restrain myself. This is a dangerous city. This man is a stranger even if he doesn't feel like one.

We approach my block. The cab glides to a stop in front of my building. I don't know what to do. I don't want this to end. One of the many idiosyncratic adventures available to any New Yorker who has enough gumption to get out of his apartment. Yet I don't want to seem too forward. All men are predators. I read that in some fashion magazine. So what do I do now?

"I am Harris Schwartzman," the dark stranger offers.

Oh, right, all men are predators. I smile.

"I am Maria." I hand him my card, not too forward. Easy prey is what he must be thinking. And for him I suppose I am.

I work among men. I have had the misfortune of failing to pick one in a timely manner. I don't find many of them that interesting. So when I find one that pleases me, restraint goes out the window. I am lonely and sex-starved and desirous of having a child. Let's go, I think. Even I find it abysmal, but I can't help it. It's what flashes the neon lights in my brain. To hell with mystery and predatory games. Let's find romance before we die. Let's make our own group so we can be fortified against all of the other groups. And let's stop being iconoclasts too. Let's get a Volvo wagon with sticky shit on the windows and animal crackers on the floor and go. Must we continue to hold out for The One?

Must we keep waiting till we win the Olympics, the Pulitzer, the Nobel, and an Emmy so we know we're ready?

I am repulsed by my own desperation as I climb out of the cab onto the snowy sidewalk. It's late. The doorman is nowhere in sight. I fish around in my bag for the front door key. I do not look back. If he calls, he calls. And if he doesn't, this incident can be added to the litany of incidents that keep me up at night. Maria-the-asshole moments. Flashes of desperation, and character flaws, and other human foibles too embarrassing to mention, but perennially available for late-night review.

JANUARY 15 The Radical Theatre Agent stops me in the hall. "Maria, I hope you have something to say at the staff meeting," he barks. I do not respond. He keeps moving.

The anger is palpable in the conference room. I walk to a side table laden with slightly stiff bagels and day-old cream cheese. The effort at fecundity is halfhearted. The message: we all need to be doing better. Too much fear leads to anger, I think as I halfheartedly plot my comments for the meeting. "Okay, we're hooked up," some technical guy comments efficiently. This is my favorite part: we teleconference with the coast. Pieces of elbow and half conversations, and then displeasure from people in a box, a projection from three thousand miles away. There is antipathy between the coasts. Everyone in Hollywood thinks New York is not signing enough, is not booking enough, is not prominent enough. And all the New Yorkers think the people on the West Coast just suck.

As I take a seat at the super-long conference table floating above midtown I think of a way of eradicating much of the anger at this table. In the New York office there is a lot of sexual confusion. My Fantasy Self stands up and clicks my glass of not so fresh o.j. "Could everyone please take out their house keys and throw them into the middle of the conference table," my Fantasy Self begins. The tall talent agent with the pronounced lisp and triplets in Darien slides his into the center of the table. "That's fine," I say, encouraging him, knowing that his anger will dissipate when I make him trade places with a short southern literary agent who lives in the West Village and can't get arrested down there. I feel a smile in my heart when I think of the squat southerner boinking the mother of the triplets and liking it. Of his new life in Darien, attending the Episcopal Church and rushing home to see the kiddies in their first school play. I'll wipe that frown from his pale visage. And his trade, I think of him happily shopping on Christopher Street. Openly enjoying the companionship of another man he can call sweetie and mean it.

Then there is the fat blonde talent agent who can't find a guy to save her life. It seems she's the only one who didn't get the memo. "Get a clue," my Fantasy Self yells into her little round ear. "You loved women's lacrosse in college." She is moved down to the Village to the apartment of an eighty-year-old secretary who hasn't had sex since 1942. We move the old secretary to the fat agent girl's Upper East Side apartment and marry her off to a recent widower mogul when he's still too distraught to realize he'd rather have a buxom twenty-eight-year-old.

As I contemplate my trades, I hover above the bitter haze enveloping the table. There may be hope, I think, buoyed by my own fantasies. And then I hear my name out of the box from California, accompanied by static, but still identifiable.

"Maria, what do you have to report?" the Grand Poo Bah Agent drones.

"I had an interesting meeting with Barry Hovington, who is in from London for the premiere of his new film," I confidently commence. "The film is fantastic. I hope you'll all get a chance to see it," I continue, thinking of drunken Barry's "fuck you" of the previous night. Thinking of him dead on his ass in some swanky hotel being paid for by the studio, still three hours from awakening to a bad old hangover with no recollection of last night. With no recollection of our encounter. I confidently proceed. "Barry and I plan to meet again before he leaves New York; he is itching for a move." Itching, my ass. Maybe scratching and pulling out his hair as the result of too much booze last night and not enough this morning. I wonder where I come up with these things. I've got to head down one flight of stairs to my office, and the little assistant and I have to find old Barry. I wish I had found out where he was staying last night. Oh, dear Lord. I settle back into my chair. They are on to the next victim, the little men in the box who claim to be Hollywood theatrical agents.

Barry and I meet that afternoon, four o'clock to be exact, at a bistro on Madison in the Sixties. The Studio has him at The Mark. He is winded from the six-block trek. He is trying to be nonchalant about the shaking.

"What do you say about a couple of Bloody Marys," I say with reassurance.

Barry's eyes slightly brighten. You're not a bad ole gal, his look seems to say. "Yes, fine," he says, trying not to seem desperate.

As I have already ordered them, they appear immediately.

I take one for show. After he downs the first one, I will quietly slide mine over. An agent must contemplate the needs of her client.

"There's quite a buzz about the film," I commence.

"Cut the crap," he intones.

"Okay," I agree. "I loved it. It's going to make a ton of money. I would like to represent you," I try again.

"Better." He nods as he downs the second Bloody and signals to the bartender to keep 'em coming. He is coming back. Alcohol is bringing him back. He is the one in control. He directs the action. I am relieved, and desperate. He is my shot at getting my contract renewed, at least that is what I believe at this moment. Without him, I am nothing.

"Why should I leave the Bozos who presently represent me?" he asks.

"Well, we have a London office," I try.

"So do I," he answers back. "Listen, my pet, do you really think I need to go sit in some agent's office?"

"No, but you deserve double the money you're making now, and meaningful back-end participation," I keep trying.

"Of course I do," he agrees. "But if my present Bozos can't get it for me why should I believe some future Bozos will?" he demands. It is a fair question.

"It will be my life's mission," I snap back, leaning forward in my chair so that our two heads are almost touching. I feel his clamminess.

He responds to my irony. "It's lucky for you I am South African, ole gal," he says and smiles. "Yanks aren't big on irony."

I have a strategic moment. I could play it straight and say I mean it, which in fact on some level I do, or I could go with the devil-may-care, if not you, then some other seven-figure director attitude. I go for a compromise.

"If you sign with us, I will make it happen," I say. "You have my word. I am not some mean boy in an Armani suit. I am smart and I am committing myself to you." I stop. It is a performance. He is a talented director. He scrutinizes me. Then downs another Bloody. More than three, less than six, I think, all the while wondering if he is buying it. He leans across the table and grabs the nipple of my right breast. He gives it a good squeeze. It is an important moment. I do not respond. I look him straight in the eye. Finally he removes his hand from my breast.

"Okay," he says. "What the fuck."

I wish I had brought signing papers to the little bistro. I need him to sign the agency contract before he gets on a plane. I don't want to make a misstep, not now. There is pounding in my ears. "How long are you in New York?"

"I leave tonight," he responds. There is a new tone in his voice. I have become a supplicant.

I have a plan. "What flight?" I casually ask.

"Ten o'clock back to London," he answers.

"British Air?" I ask, trying to be nonchalant.

"Yes," he says.

I have still not mentioned the papers. Closing is an all-important aspect of any deal. I need to get this fucker to sign on the dotted line, and yet I don't want to spook him. And I don't want to give him a choice.

"I'll messenger the papers to the hotel," I say, as we are standing outside the bistro in the cold January light.

"Fine," he responds. He leans down to kiss me good-bye, and

as I look up in preparation for a peck on the cheek he slides his darting tongue into my unwilling mouth. I respond slightly. I need him and he knows it. He's tested this thesis for himself, the breast, the mouth. I will be ever devoted and he will continually try and take advantage—another Tacit Agreement.

My assistant and I get right to work executing the necessary documents. I love my assistant. He is compact, refined, thorough, and on his way to Harvard Business School. Someday he'll look back and laugh at all of this, but for now he treats the tasks at hand respectfully. I slap two hundred bucks in his hand. "See if you can catch him at The Mark and get him to sign; if not, take a cab to the airport. His flight is British Airways number 60."

"No problem." Jed, the assistant, smiles. His teeth are white and regular.

"You're the greatest," I say.

"I know," he says, rolling his eyes. My superlative style grates on more than just him, but in a half-assed sort of way I do mean all of this shit and Jed knows that too.

"Call me from the road," I yell as he heads down the long narrow hall, agents in their offices on one side, assistants in their cubicles on the other. He does not answer. He just keeps going out and down and over to find the South African and "facilitate" his signing.

I am manning the operation alone. Not too tough. We have caller ID. There is no way I am going to speak to one out-of-work client today. It rings, I look, and my voice mail picks up. My heart goes out to them alone in their rooms, jobless, money running out, but I need to be free to call future employers, not waste time adding salve to their wounded egos. If I had a friggin' job for them, believe me I'd have called.

The phone rings again, this time a number I do not recognize. What the hell. I pick it up.

"Hello," I say in an officious, I-am-so-busy-I-have-four-lines-going sort of way.

"Is this the office of Maria O'Mara?" the voice asks.

"Yes," I answer, not identifying myself.

"This is Harris Schwartzman, is she in?" My dark handsome stranger.

"One moment," I say, disguising my voice by holding my nose. I put him on hold. I am glad and scared. I run a comb through my hair and apply some lip gloss, then pick the receiver back up. "Hello," I say in a slightly drawn-out way.

"Hi," my dark stranger responds.

"So . . . ," I say. I know how to fill airwaves, I am a friggin' agent, but I am not prepared to tap-dance here. Not now. I chased you in the snow. I hitched a cab ride. Now you do something.

"So you want to go to a movie?" he asks.

"Sure," I answer.

"How 'bout tonight?" This is my problem. I always give in too soon. And I've got Jed running all over hell. I need to be reachable. I refuse to bring a cell phone to our first date.

"Sorta got a work drama going on," I say with importance, but sweetly. Letting him know I am a professional with a lot on my plate, but sweet too.

"Oh," he says. He is clearly disappointed. There is too much silence.

Finally, I take the bait. "Shall we make a plan?"

"Yeah, sure, how about tomorrow?" he asks hopefully. Maybe he is just nice and lonely. I look at my calendar, nothing for a Wednesday night.

"Great," I say.

"I'll call tomorrow," he continues.

"Okay, bye," I say. Maybe my life will work out. If Barry signs, and this Harris thing turns into something, I will have pulled it out of my hat once again. I do a little dance around my desk and sit back down. It's never good to get too happy, I remember. Now whom can I call? The phone rings. It's Jed. I am scared, but I pick it up anyway.

"We got it," Jed says proudly, referring to Barry's signed agency contract. It is what I need to hear.

JANUARY 16 I am standing in the bar of the most chic Italian restaurant in the West Village. New York City is the land of restaurant achievement and I have arrived. At least at this particular moment, thanks to the short dark stranger. Because I am here I believe he is intrigued. I am worried I have on all of the wrong clothes. The minute he arrives I know I am right. His look of disappointment stings. I will charm him back. I chide myself for self-destructive impulses that have led me to wear wool slacks, a cashmere sweater, and comfortable Gucci loafers on a bitterly cold night.

"Hey," he says a little stiffly as we crowd ourselves further into the bar area of the brightly lit restaurant. Our eyes meet. He is shorter and more compact then I remember. "Do you want a drink?" he continues in less than convincing tones.

"I'll wait," I say in deference to his ambivalence.

His arms are too short and there are beads of perspiration around his thick black eyebrows. It seems as if he can barely stand the wait. Hey, buddy, this is no endurance contest, I long to say. And then just when I think all is lost he flashes a wonderful smile.

"So much for reservations," he says and shrugs as our bodies mash up against each other, and even more people are herded into the little bar area. His breath is sweet. His eyelashes are long and black and thick as a child's. I try an appealing shoulder throw, accompanied by a subtle pout. He flashes me a half smile.

I am always denying that I am selling sex, but dating is marketing, and now I am down several points. Stiletto heels and a short skirt were what was called for—and then denial. These paradigms we live by are all so clear. There is really no excuse for failure. I fear I am compelled by my weakened position. Now the race is on. Can I make him love me when he is not sure he wants me? I have set a goal for myself. My own perversity contravenes the natural order of things. I am an agent. I like the chase. But no man worth his salt wants to be pursued. He wants to do the chasing. And so I am perpetually caught, being chased and rejecting, or chasing and being rejected.

These first dates are always testing grounds and forums for showing off. He is ordering our food in Italian. He has taken over, and I am glad. I start my own performance.

"Did you ever notice that it is equally important to be both wraithlike and eating at the most superb restaurants in this city?" I begin with a paradox that has been gnawing away at me at least for an hour and a half—that is, since I was finding it difficult to button my trousers tonight.

The dark one looks at me blankly. This is not a tune he feels like humming. I decide it would be best not to question his choices. I become quiet and wait. I have a friend who says that in order for a woman to get a man she must disappear. Call me Houdini. I say nothing. I try just smiling.

"I dated Missy Fisher," he blurts out. He feels the need to confess he has dated someone I know vaguely out in L.A.

"That doesn't matter." I smile. He breathes a sigh of relief.

"She just didn't get me," he says. I nod knowingly. Will I? I wonder.

"This Barolo hails from Piemonte—Piedmont," he translates. "It is produced on a family estate." Who knew? I try and seem interested as he attempts to educate me about his wine selection. He is animated and false in an A-student-giving-a-report-to-the-class sort of way. His posture connotes pride.

"After Stanford, I traveled extensively, and one day I knew I was meant to tell people's truths," he reveals. People from good schools are like lesbians and Catholics—always bringing up membership in the first five minutes of conversation.

"That's the day I became a journalist," he continues. Although he produces a reality television show, he considers himself a journalist. "Our show is really about human nature."

As he fills the airwaves I assess my situation.

1. Limited number of fertile eggs
2. Overdue to make a score in the man department
3. Potential blowout on the career front
4. Employed, age-appropriate Stanford grad at close range
5. Conclusion: this must be IT.

"Encountering foreign cultures really opened me up," he continues. I try to listen to his words, but I am focused on our quadruplets, the result of fertility drugs, all healthy, all boys,

Nicholas, Harry, Max, and Sam Schwartzman. They look charming harnessed into my fictional black Mercedes SUV.

The thought of Harris, our boys, and myself produces a distinct sensation. I spend so much time suppressing my own sexual drive, the mere thought of reproduction seems to have started the works. "Chug-a-lug," scream my ovaries. "Let's move on this one."

"I loved living in Paris," he informs. "That city had more influence over who I am than any other factor in my life." I nod as he reveals his truths, but I am too excited to focus on his words. I ingest the fine red wine. If he proposes tonight I will only be ten years behind schedule.

"Maria," he says as we stand on the sidewalk in the bitter cold, not one cab in sight.

"Yes?" I reply, wondering about his expectations. There is a slight hesitation, and then he is leaning forward, pressing his lips against mine. And then another pause as he waits to see my reaction. Not the proposal I am looking for, but a proposal. This is the tricky part. I try to summon every magazine article and self-help book I have ever perused on this topic, be friendly and rejecting.

"Shall I kiss you again?" he whispers. And then we do. I feel his body's warmth, and I am floating. But I can't. Where are the 1950s when you need them?

I am safe, I think, as I step into the elevator of my building alone. I enter my apartment. I pull off my clothes and take refuge in my bed, reassured by the weight of the two comforters I have piled on top of myself. I seem to remember a thought I have never had, that the only time you can really have someone is when you don't need them. I promise myself to become someone who doesn't need Harris. I believe I may have finally cracked this pairing-off thing. I am delighted about the kissing, and pleased to have decided upon a strategy.

JANUARY 22 "Maria, I want you to trade offices with Bingham," snaps The Radical Theatre Agent en route to lunch.

"But why?" I question in a slight whine, suddenly feeling very attached to my cramped four-walled office.

"Department decision," he brusquely responds, explaining nothing.

"But it makes no sense," I try again.

"Just do it," he commands. This is it. Whenever they're going to fire you they first take the opportunity to assert their power over you.

Bingham is an addict. Her most recent transgression: falling asleep in a signing meeting. She is definitely getting sacked; that is, if she doesn't drop dead first. The reason they haven't fired her yet is because she has a loyal client-base of well-knowns. Never good to ruffle the moneymaking feathers. What purpose could it possibly serve for us to trade offices?

Jed and I walk into Bingham's office—old shoes, piles of coffee-stained, dog-eared scripts, a refrigerator brimming with unrecognizable bearded food. I watch as Jed carefully steps over a patch of greenish black mold cultured in the center of the carpet.

"This is scary," I comment as I pick up a lone high heel encrusted in a foreign substance I would rather not identify.

"No one from the mail room will even come in here," says Jed. "They just leave her mail outside the door," he explains as he clears a path through a heap of trash.

"Hey, honey," exclaims Sean, my very stylish gay agent pal. "I hear you're moving."

"What did they do, announce it over the P.A.?" I demand. He steps gingerly across the threshold. "Welcome to the Bacteria Motel." I wince as I remove my arm from a slimy wall.

"This space has definite potential," he encourages. I'm intent upon hiding my hysteria. "If I were you I would be proactive. Have the evil spirits removed. You, my friend, need a clearing," he advises. And then he sashays out.

"I definitely need a clearing," I say to Jed, who nods affirmatively, trying to seem nonjudgmental, all the while clearly projecting his Connecticut values onto each idiosyncratic situation that arises.

The phone in Bingham's office rings, and suddenly a familiar voice wafts through the office.

"I've got my cock in my hand," the well-known movie star explains.

"Oh, my God," I mouth to Jed. We are both transfixed.

"I am thinking of that blow job you gave me in the cab last

night. Oh, Jesus, I am so excited," he continues rather emphatically.

Neither Jed nor I breathe. That's cheating. No wonder she has such a good client list.

"Bingham, baby, are you there?" the movie star demands plaintively.

"Uh-huh," answers Jed in a high-pitched falsetto. I love my assistant.

"Oh, Bingham, I am going to come," he screams and then a *click*.

"I'll get some boxes sent up," Jed says.

"Great, and let's make sure the phone lines are properly transferred," I add.

"Will do."

New York City provides. Felissimo is a magical department store on West Fifty-sixth Street. Laden with elegant treasures and staffed with tarot card readers in its tearoom—it is certainly worth a try.

"Hello, yes, I'm looking for someone to do a clearing," I start rather tentatively.

"But of course, madame," the woman on the other end of the line reassures. "I have just the man for you. He's a genius." Helium will meet me in the office this evening for a clearing and a blessing at 10 P.M. He insists I run home and take a bath in goat's milk in the interim.

"No call from the mystery date, but three from Barry," Jed reports toward the end of the day.

"Better not let him know about Bingham's level of service or I am screwed," I retort.

"He really wants that movie at Universal," Jed reminds me.

"I know," I say through gritted teeth. "He wants the job and double the money. And that's what I promised him I could do," I acknowledge dismally.

"You'll get it," Jed says encouragingly.

I review my call sheet without looking up. "I am going home for a bit before a late meeting in the office," I say.

"Should I stay?" Jed asks worriedly.

"Not necessary," I reply as he hands me my order from the bodega downstairs—canned milk and flowers.

I am soaking in goat's milk laced with fresh daisies. I feel my grasp at the agency weakening. The signs are clear. The vultures are circling. But at least I am being proactive. I am meeting my shaman at ten. At this point I will try anything to hold on to my job. Still no call from Harris. I could kill myself for not dressing like a slut. Could the kisses have felt less wonderful to him? I always wonder about this. If you think it's great, is it still possible the other party is disappointed?

I try to give the high sign to the guard downstairs as Helium and I sign in to the building.

"We should be down in an hour," I loudly state, trying to signal that if we are not, the proper authorities should be called. When our eyes finally meet, the guard seems bored and unaware of this potentially lethal situation.

Helium and I head up to the nineteenth floor. He has long hair, is balding on the top, and carries a large attaché case. I would like to ask him how he got into this line of work, but his sharp, discolored teeth make me less inclined toward conversation. I notice he has a limp.

"I did the goat's milk thing," I offer. He does not respond. I lead him toward my office.

"Your present space?" he asks.

"Yes, this is my office," I say, clearly articulating each syllable. I am not really sure what I am dealing with here.

"Oh, I see," he says in a worried tone. "And your future space?" I show him to Bingham's office. He scowls. "There is a lot of darkness here," he says grimly.

"A lot?" I question. Now I am really worried.

"Yes," he responds as he begins to pull an unending number of feathers, marbles, and crystals from his pants pockets. From his coat he pulls out the longest long scarf I have ever encountered and several incense twigs. He dexterously reassembles his attaché case into a makeshift altar, which he sets up on Bingham's recently cleared desk. He lights the incense, and then begins to chant. "Omm," he skillfully expels.

"Yes, I feel much heaviness here. You definitely need a clearing," he continues. He hands me a pair of finger cymbals and places a feather behind my left ear. "Now chant om," he instructs.

As this is costing me four hundred bucks I do as told. "Ommmm," I chant until I can't expel any more air from my lungs as I clash the little symbols.

Suddenly, Helium sprays me with holy water followed by glittery multicolored sparkle dust. I sense the sparkles adhering to my moistened skin. I feel ridiculous and desperate—a bad combination. "Oh, my God," I mutter under my breath.

"Excuse me?" says Helium.

"Nothing," I say.

By now he has lit several candles and is jumping from one foot to the other and making a nasal sound, which emanates from his mouth. He nods in my direction. Now I am hopping from foot to foot attempting to replicate his nasal uttering. If this will save my ass I will stand here and jump all night.

"Native American smudge bundles for prosperity," he explains as he lights two sagebrush torches and hands me one. "Come," he instructs.

We parade up and down the darkened agency halls dressed in our feathers and tightly gripping our smoking sage.

"We bless this entire sacred place and all who toil here," Helium emphatically calls out. And then an encouraging nod. "We bless this sacred place and all who toil here," we call out together. This is definitely an aerobic workout. The endorphins are kicking in. My mood lightens. Helium sprays holy water on each of my colleagues' office doors. Billowing smoke fills the hallway and then miraculously—the lights. It really is working.

"What the fuck?" Julius, the head of business affairs, screams in our direction.

"We smelled smoke," his assistant, Jamalle, adds as they get perilously close. Jamalle ascertains the situation. "It's a clearing dude," he proudly surmises.

"Right," I say, holding my head up high. "We're bringing prosperity to the agency."

"Well, put out the fires, would ya?" Julius commands, trying not to seem ruffled.

Helium and I walk back to my office, both trying to make as little of this encounter as possible. "Wow, you certainly handled that," exclaims the startled shaman.

"Yeah," I say. Helium and I are really bonding.

"You knew just what to say to that guy."

"Well, you know, it's an agency," I say with a shrug, quite sure that old Helium and I have just hammered the final nail into my unemployment coffin. What the hell? I am educated. I'll find another job—at least I hope I will.

JANUARY 24 The imminent demise of life as I know it has sent me right to Manolo Blahnik to purchase a pair of five-hundred-dollar high heels. That, and my second date with Harris planned for tonight. A Thursday night date, not a Friday or a Saturday, but not a Sunday afternoon either. It could be worse. I wonder if it is unrealistic to think I can be engaged to be married and running a Fortune 500 company before my contract is up. Seventy-two days and counting—not impossible, I think as I hungrily caress a second pair of shoes. I've got to use some restraint. New York City with all of its quickness just keeps delivering the bad news. Fun City is for the rich and powerful. If you're not part of the solution you've definitely got a problem.

For our second date Harris comes as a younger, more ebullient version of himself. He's wearing some kind of sports clothes. Not a riding-to-the-hounds type of getup, more like a South American rugby situation. We make quite a pair: Pia Zadora meets Wayne Gretsky circa 1985. My shoes are so high I can barely navigate, which isn't a completely bad thing because my skirt is so short I probably would be arrested if I bent even slightly.

"We're going to stop by my friends', the Kaygels, for dinner," Harris informs me as we meet on the street at an appointed location outside a diner on West Fifty-seventh Street.

This is great. I am dressed like a hooker. A perfect time to meet the friends.

"I thought we'd walk, but you'll never make it in those shoes," Harris remarks in an annoyed manner as he rushes into the street and hails a cab.

Thanks for the heads-up. I thought we were doing an intimate *dîner à deux*, and the next thing I know I am being ushered into a fabulous park-view apartment on Fifth Avenue.

It seems that the criterion for an invitation to this dinner is good looks. In Los Angeles there are no unattractive people, but in New York, where individuality and intelligence are prized traits, not everyone is necessarily beautiful. Harris's friends are the beautiful, well-educated set. The talk revolves around sports, travel, each other, and food. It seems everyone here runs marathons and eats. And they all know exactly the same people.

When we are all finally amassed and seated at the long dining room table our number comes to twenty-five. Here is an apartment of Louis Quatorze proportions. Some decorator has had a field day. The furnishings are an eclectic mix of periods with examples of the most expensive items from each, displayed merrily. Harris is seated so far away from me I can barely see him. I shift to agent mode. So much for the date; this is just another gig. I shall work the room.

"I am Maria O'Mara," I say to the man on my right.

"Finber O'Shaunessy," the little man answers in a thick Irish brogue. He has that I'll-make-this-fun-if-it-kills-me Irish charm thing going. Relax, buddy, I come from the same school. It doesn't need to be so much fun. "I am Harris's best friend. They sat me here to get the lowdown," he says with a smile, as he peers down into my lap where my skirt has risen so high on my thighs that I am afraid to look. The view doesn't seem to be bothering Fin, not one bit.

"This is quite an apartment," I comment to get the conversation flowing.

"Bruce inherited it," Finber informs me.

"Did his parents live here?" I ask.

"Oh, you don't know the story?" Finber, somewhat surprised, gamely inquires. There it is again, this context thing. It would never occur to anyone in attendance that you don't know all of their friends and acquaintances. An image of a small child strolling down the aisle of a supermarket comes to mind. It never occurs to the child that just because his mother is several aisles over she cannot hear him telling her what sugar-coated cereal he desires. I am here therefore I must know Bruce and his story. Oh, well, an oversight; the little Irishman takes it in stride, happy enough to get the gossip rolling. "No, no, not his parents. His wife—his dead wife, I should say." He's off and running now, the little leprechaun with a good story.

"Oh, I am sorry," I say just to participate.

"No, no, it's a fine thing, she was ninety-five," he continues. I think Bruce is the overweight forty-something with the moist hands who greeted me in the foyer. I am a little off balance now. This makes the storyteller gleeful. He continues. "You see, after Harvard, Bruce didn't really have any direction so he came to New York and started a dog-walking business."

I nod. Harvard, dogs, sure, it makes sense.

"Lavinia had four, no, maybe five Afghans. They loved Bruce. He moved in. They got married. She died. And now he is a member of the co-op board." Fin winks. Nice and neat, I think, at the same time realizing it was probably anything but.

"And Bruce is with . . . ?" I begin the question fully aware that all questions will be answered.

"Bruce is married to Catherine—you know, the pregnant decorator—and they have two adopted Chinese daughters, Emerald and Patience."

I peer down the table at our round hostess, whose hair is a shade of red that can only come from a bottle. And her hairdresser would be . . . ? Months ago I would have said this aloud, but I am working this situation. I need a score. I've got to marry this one and if his friends are part of the package so be it.

To my left is a diminutive woman nearing seventy. It appears they have seated all of the short people at this end.

"I am Maria," I begin.

"Lillian, Cecilia's mother," the woman tersely explains. I am not even going to ask her who Cecilia is; I am on information overload and Lillian clearly is in on the conspiracy. You're here, so of course you know Cecilia and all of her intricacies, her glance connotes. I nod knowingly, grateful for the soup that has been placed before me.

Several courses later I feel two hands on my shoulders. There is a combination of intimacy and ownership to this gesture that I have only longed for until now.

"Get up," Harris commands into the back of my head. I do as I am told. He grasps my hand with his own with precisely the same amount of pressure he was applying to my shoulders. I feel

I am being infused with affection. I hope this sensation is more than just the wine. As the others cleanse their palettes he leads me off into a darkened hallway. He motions for hushed tones and tentatively opens a door. We move inside. There is just enough light from somewhere down the hall to illuminate two sleeping children.

"Emerald and Patience?" I whisper.

Harris smiles. He stands behind me and wraps his arms across my body. We watch them sleep, two very lonely forty-year-olds watching two safe children, very far from their homeland.

As we ride home in the cab, the thought occurs to me that the sleeping children thing is his move. This is only the second date. I've got to hold out at least until date three; date five would be better. I loathe my conflict.

"I am going to go home," I say, once again revealing too much. He has not invited me to his place. He has not suggested that he would like to join me in mine. I wonder if I will ever learn to just say nothing. Harris nods. He is careful and quiet. I turn slightly to look into his eyes, to see if I am pretty enough. And then I can't bear to look. So I close my eyes and we kiss. And then I am alone on the sidewalk, heading for the door, not looking back and unsure.

JANUARY 28 The phone is screaming at me to pick it up and deliver good news. I am definitely having a bad face day, which is so much worse than a bad hair day because it is impossible to just put your face in a ponytail and forget about it. And there is the small matter of Harris not calling all weekend, definitely not a promising sign. It feels as if it will be impossible to turn this awful Monday around. I pray for luck, even the smallest sign.

Jed keeps buzzing me, and I keep motioning a big fat *No*. Every client is calling to see what job I got them over the weekend. They are not paying me 10 percent of their annual income for me to tell them I stayed in bed most of Saturday, getting out only once to bathe and once more to receive takeout. That in fact I did not finish reading one of their screenplays although I started seven of them. Nor would they be eager to hear about my Sunday, my run around the reservoir, drop-in at the Met, and uninspired dinner for one of leftover takeout.

I try to imagine why each client believes that news of his career will be any different Monday at 10 A.M. from what it was Friday at 5 P.M. In fact, even if I had gone to a treacherous dinner party of producers and studio executive types not much would have changed. But had I gone to such a dinner or a movie premiere I would have had access to that all-important Show Biz commodity—information. And if I had the information, then I could certainly convert it to money, opportunity, and fame on the client's behalf and I would have finally earned my 10 percent.

"You've gotta take this. It's Barry Hovington's third call from Provence, and he's pissed," Jed says through gritted teeth.

"Really, really pissed?" I ask with a wicked smile.

"Yep," Jed replies. He is clearly tired of fielding calls.

"Hullo, Barry," I say in a long, drawn-out, agent sort of way.

"Cut the crap and never avoid me," Barry retorts. I guess he really is pissed. "I want to fly to Hollywood and pitch a movie idea."

"Yes?" I say.

"I've had the most inspired notion," he claims. Barry is a director whose work I really do admire. I am poised to hear the idea. This may be the thing that turns this Monday around.

"A naked man runs across the city," he says, quite proud of himself.

This is a tricky moment. Is this a put-on—do I laugh? Or is he serious? The agent is the parent. The client is always testing.

"Elaborate," I say, trying to sound interested, yet reserved. He is from a country that was once part of the British Empire; reserved is definitely the stance here.

"Don't you see it?" he screams. "Uptight businessman, important meeting, fucking around on the wife, gets locked out of the hotel, buck naked. There is a naked man loose in the city.

Fucking brilliant, don't you think?" I imagine that Barry is cheating on his stout British wife in Provence, got locked out of his hotel room, and now it's art, or at least a Hollywood movie deal.

"So you want to pitch it to all of the heavy hitters?" I say with as much animation as possible.

"Precisely!" he screams. Henry Higgins—*By George, she's got it. She's finally got it!*

"I'll set up the meetings. When do you want to go?" I ask.

"Soon!" he screams.

I imagine Barry floating into smoggy Hollywood manning the hot air balloon I have arranged for him. The French girlfriend pops her head up out of the basket. "She's just along for the ride," he giggles. "He'll be landing at three o'clock," I advise some middle-level executive over the phone. "Just look out your window," I tell him. "Oh, my God, he's buck naked," Mr. Middle Level exclaims. "Maria, you've done it again." "I know," my Fantasy Self says with all of the bravado of an Armani suit. "I am good."

The Radical Theatre Agent appears at my door.

"I am going out with a pitch," I say meekly.

"Good for you," he snaps. "Listen, you need to go home and change." I stare at him. I feel I dress impeccably. "Otto Wokoff needs an escort for that premiere thing tonight," he continues. Otto Wokoff is that weird character actor. He scares people. Rumor has it he's got a major drug problem. "There's a dinner afterward and every agent in town will be there. Stick close," The Radical Theatre Agent commands.

"I'll bring my sword," I say.

The Radical Theatre Agent whisks off down the hall.

The game is never to let the client engage with an agent from another agency. The client might bond during mindless dinner chatter. And then he will leave. While it is true that agents from rival agencies are constantly calling others' successful clients, the humiliation of having one stolen right out from under your nose must be avoided at all cost.

I speed uptown on the B train. Shower and change in a record fifteen minutes, and hit the street. Not a doorman in sight. Certainly no taxis. A surge of panic. If I am late The Radical Theatre Agent will find out and will do worse than fire me. My hands become clammy. There is nothing worse than sweaty black-tie. I make a run for the crosstown bus. "How ya doin', Cinderella?" the bus driver snickers as I search for change in the smallest evening bag ever designed.

"Won't you just take two dollar bills?" I beg.

He points to the sign: CHANGE ONLY. I am about to lose my shit on the crosstown bus.

"Come here," a large African American woman orders, with just the proper amount of disdain. She grabs my two dollars and hands me eight quarters.

"Thanks," I say. She does not respond.

Kaplink, kaplink, kaplink, kaplink, kaplink, kaplink, kaplink, kaplink. I am on and paid for. I settle into the reassurance of the seat. I wish I could stay on the bus forever or at least until my life is settled. The motion transports me to a meditative state. My thoughts float at a safe distance.

"Get off!" the bus driver and the African American woman scream. Jarred, I do as I am told. I make a soft landing onto Fifth Avenue and attempt a high-heeled run.

Winded but on time, I hit the red carpet just paces behind Otto. He seems fine as I maneuver closer to let him know I am here. When I am next to him I gently touch his elbow.

"I am Maria O'Mara, one of your agents," I say.

"No touching!" he barks.

I am stunned. "Okay," I say.

His lips seem to be turning blue. He is clearly agitated as we make our way. He lowers his ten-foot body into his reserved seat.

"Would you care for some water?" I ask.

"No," he groans.

I can't wait for the dinner. Perhaps we can dance without touching, the Touchless Tango. Finally the movie is over. And then the rush of bodies. We walk across the street to the Plaza. Plenty of photographs and no touching. The dinner is grim. No touching, no talking, no dessert. Finally, Red Botticelli, Otto's principal agent, shows.

"I didn't know about the touching," I whisper.

"Yeah, no touching," he reiterates.

"No shit," I say. Red moves proprietarily toward Otto.

This premiere is one of many co-opted by a charity. Tonight all of the non-show-business types have paid through the nose to support after-school sports in New York's inner city. I want to raise my hand and be called upon by Miriam Whomever, this year's chair. I would sidle up to the dais. "Yes, I just want to remind all of the celebrities here tonight to try and act normal," I would commence. "I know you are overpaid and have people like myself attempting to cater to your every whim, but try to remember when you were a kid who just liked to engage in after-school sports"—it is good to have a tie-in—"when you only dreamed of being lauded at events like this. Think about it and then think about trying to act like an insurance agent or a driving instructor, or a dentist, and we will all be better off. Thank you and good night," I would say.

"Maria!" someone yells from across the room, knocking me from my reverie. It is a kid turned movie star I grew up with in Los Angeles. He flies over, finally having a purpose in a room full of strangers. "Maria!" he screams again as he lifts me out of my chair and gives me an overacted smack on the lips. Old Otto smiles at me as if we were best buddies. Yeah now. He probably would even let me touch him.

"Hey," I say, basking in this momentary glory and hating myself all in the same moment.

Old Actor Boy puts his arm around me and assumes an intimate whisper pose. "How are your mom and brother?" he importantly asks as photographers snap away.

"Great," I whisper back, thinking I really should call my family. It's been weeks. And then out of nowhere Harris appears. The same dumb grin as Otto's is plastered across Harris's face. My heart starts pounding.

I have this theory that all of the people you are meant to be around are around you at all times, and often you just don't notice them. But I am noticing now. I assume the intimate whisper pose myself, and ask Actor Boy a question. "How long are you in New York?"

He nods as if considering my profound thoughts. More camera clicks. "Leaving in the morning," he finally whispers back, meaningfully squeezing my hand in his. Flashing a grin for the one lone celebrity photographer still clicking. "I'll call you," he says as a posse of agents from his agency descends upon the table and is literally pulling him away. I am having so many victories at this moment I have to stop to calculate just how many, but I can't. There is the matter of Harris still panting in my face.

"Big supporter of after-school sports?" I inquire. I will not mention that he did not call over the weekend, after our second date. I do take notice of the fact that this is the second premiere party I have seen him at in the short time I have known him.

There is a species of single men in New York who actively score tickets to big events. Since there is practically an event a night for nine months out of the year, a lot of their workday is spent hustling tickets. I am not sure exactly what fuels their actions—social ambition, professional ambition, wanting to get laid by an actress, any combination of these are all plausible theories. Maybe they just want to be a part of it (spelled capital IT). The IT being the social/celebrity swirl by which a lot of New York defines itself. I have always found these men odious. I suppose because I am at odds with this aspect of my own character. I am an agent. I kiss ass and go to these functions for a living. I must prove daily that I am a part of IT, and somehow I must translate that into jobs—i.e., cold hard cash for writers, directors, and actors.

Harris is clearly not the Nobel laureate fantasy husband. He is on the make. He produces a silly reality television show where those desirous of their fifteen minutes eat bugs or smoosh bird poop into their hair. But I am attracted to him.

"The network bought a table," he says and shrugs. "How do you know What's-His-Name?"

There it is, the zillion-dollar question. How do I know some kid from high school who turned out to be a big star? I am wearing the magic fairy dust and Harris wants to lick it off. It would have been so much cooler if he had not inquired after the star. Down another five points.

"Show business," I answer, hanging on to my tenuous power. Turning a little in the light so he can see all the secondhand sparkle. I chide myself for not introducing Harris to What's-His-Name. Harris would have loved it and at least I could still like myself for holding on to some social grace.

We are fumbling in Harris's loft-style apartment. Even in the dark I can tell it is perfect, industrial design, not a sock out of place. Granite countertops in the kitchen are a certainty. Not Martha Stewart, but her daughter would love the place. This is his lair. The style gleaned from reading too many *New York* magazines.

Harris is aroused. He is unbuttoning the shirt of an intimate of a movie star. And once again I am giving in to loneliness, to sexual desire, and to the faint hope that I can convert this to love and marriage and kids who go to a posh Hamptons day camp. I try and repress the patina of superficiality that sticks to both of us like gum. I try to believe that between our animal desire and fate there is something more meaningful than our combined consciousness permits. I am being held by the short dark stranger and it feels good.

JANUARY 29 Even if I could find a cab, which I can't, there is something right about descending into the subway station in my gown and heels. Harris's face leaning over me plays over and over in my head.

"I am going running," he reported at 6 A.M.

"Okay," I replied out of the sleep zone, lying in the strange bed, waiting for the door to slam so I could get up and get out. Going running—curt but to the point. Get out of my bed. I am finished with you. If you offer yourself to the predator he cannot appreciate you.

I feel the raw taste in my mouth as I enter the uptown train. An African American woman in a crisp nurse's uniform gives me a glare. An older, fat white guy who gets on at the next stop, a knowing smile. I busily search for a place in my brain where I can file this and forget it. If I really want to marry this one why did I give in? I wonder if he'll call? How fun to see who rides the train circa 6 A.M.

It is a struggle to ascend the steep stairs to the street, but I refuse to take my heels off in the dirty subway station. I feel the muscles in my legs working for the burn. I will make a big deal at work today. *Ka-ching*. That will make the emptiness inside of me disappear. At this moment life seems to be a succession of small regrets. I guess at some point they all add up to one big long one.

Freddie the doorman greets me with a smile. "Been to a party?" he questions in his thick Spanish accent.

"Several," I say in a long drawn-out imitation Audrey Hepburn. The trick here is to keep my head held high, in an I-have-been-dancing-till-the-sun-came-up kind of way. Isn't life grand? Don't you too wish you were just arriving home in your black-tie attire? The elevator door slams shut. I am alone in the little teak room. I often wonder, when I am in here, if I may be dead and just not know it.

There is a pause when I walk into Michael's. At first I think it is my due, then my imagination, but when the maitre d' seats me there are definitely people looking. Maybe the vitamins have finally kicked in; maybe it's the new shampoo. A producer I can barely stand slides into the seat of my would-be luncheon companion who is now twenty minutes late.

"Is it true?" he asks.

"Could be," I say coyly, not having the faintest notion what he is talking about.

"Oh, come on, Maria. Is J. C. Izod attached to your Hovington pitch?" he asks.

"I've heard that," I say, hanging on to the truth by a thread. I just heard it from him, this moment. Finally my luncheon companion shows, and the sweaty producer runs off to make a call on his cell phone.

"People think we've attached J. C. Izod to the pitch," I smile and say to Jed as I walk in from lunch.

"Fifty-two calls in the last hour." He smiles back. Jed and I have been casually spreading this rumor for days. He whispering to other assistants. Me "accidentally" mentioning it to a few strategic know-it-alls.

The Radical Theatre Agent parades into my office. "So?" he says, his lips curling in the direction of a smile. "Rumors fly."

"All true," I say, again holding on to a tendril of the truth. All true that the rumors fly—undoubtedly. All true that J. C. Izod even knows of the pitch—doubtful. But if potential buyers think the biggest comedic talent in the business wants to play the role or is even thinking about it, it is sold. A slam dunk.

The Radical Theatre Agent takes his leave. I grab for the phone. "Barry, it's Maria here," I begin. "Go buy a ticket to L.A. I am setting up ten pitches a day for three days. Are you up to it?" I ask, a little afraid.

"Of course, old girl," he slurs. It is way past cocktail hour in London. I am in a racecar barreling toward a conflagration. I continue to put pressure on the accelerator.

"Great," I say and slam down the phone. "Let's start dialing," I scream out to Jed. The more I deny that the comedian is definitely attached the more everyone thinks I am lying.

FEBRUARY 8 The parking garage is cold and hollow. Harris and I are here to pick up my BMW, a souvenir from my Hollywood days. We are headed to his country house in the Hamptons for the weekend. He is very excited about the car. He has an old Jeep he keeps in the country. He doesn't have one in the city and now he does, sort of. Quite frankly, the whole car thing has been a turning point in our relationship.

"We're here to pick up our car," Harris informs the surly manager, Juan.

"Where is your ticket, baby?" Juan jets back with a glance.

"It's a monthly," Harris tries to explain. Juan remains inert. "It's my girlfriend's car," Harris tries again.

Juan's eyes speed past Harris. "Maria, *cómó está?*" he asks me.

"Bien," I reply.

Juan does one of those screeching whistles with two fingers inserted into his mouth. An underling scurries for my car, and now I am a girlfriend.

"We're having a dinner party tomorrow night," Harris informs me as we sit in heavy traffic on the Long Island Expressway. And before I can respond to that, "What do you want to prepare?" he asks. What is he talking about? I don't cook. But then again, I am interviewing for the Wife position. So what do I think I want to prepare?

"How many guests?" I inquire demurely.

"Eight for sure, perhaps twelve," he continues. Oh, my God. I have never made dinner for twelve people in my friggin' life.

"What about something French and straightforward?" I try. "You know—I'll roast a couple of chickens, some potatoes, a couple of vegetables." Who the hell do I think I am, Julia Child?

Harris's face falls. It is clear he was thinking of something more complicated. He wants tricks. I take note.

I have always tried to make up for any domestic inadequacies in the bedroom, but clearly this Wife thing is a competitive event. For my freestyle event I will give a technically superior blow job, but the compulsories, that is an entirely different matter. A roast pork, perfectly executed meringue, ironed linens, this is the real thing. As we ride along in silence my hands become clammy. My resolve is strong. I will inch toward this goal as I have inched toward so many, with painstaking determination.

FEBRUARY 9 The house is now clean. I am in charge of cleaning. He is in charge of trimming the hedges. He has gone for a run. I am rolling out the dough for an apple pie. Cooking is merely following directions and applying heat. At least that is what I keep telling myself as the hours peel away and the dinner, which has now grown to eleven, maybe twelve, looms. It seems I am happier baking and cleaning than trying to manufacture jobs and fame, but it may be a novelty thing. I think I love Harris. He wants to see if I can pull off the dinner. He liked the vacuuming.

I am trying and he is in the front yard taking a piss. I watch him through the kitchen window. I refuse to question any of this. I am tired of the solitary confinement of my life. I have my toe in the door, and I plan to keep selling. I am not sure when it happened, this shift from buyer to seller, but I am quite sure it exists. I deal with the constraints of selling every day and now I must apply my acquired expertise to my personal life. Perhaps that is where all of this has been leading. If the entire biological imperative is reproduction and all of life is constant evolution, maybe women in the twenty-first century are merely learning new tricks to capture a mate and reproduce. I place the pie in the oven and start in on peeling the potatoes. I hear Harris walk in the front door. The kitchen smells of apples. I plaster on a look of contentment.

The definite star of the dinner party is the woman with a chain of handbag stores. "All are her original design," her young toady husband explains as his manicured nails tear into the fresh peasant loaf I drove all the way to East Hampton to purchase.

Harris has placed an abundance of white candles in every room in the house and chosen a particularly nice white wine. I am glad he reads all of those food magazines. It's *Runner's World* I am still having a problem with. I try to assert myself in the proper wifely way, milling about in mules and a crisp white shirt tucked into navy capri pants, carving the chicken with confidence right at the table, and holding my gaze just a fraction of a second too long as each guest speaks. I am really interested, I try to project as they talk about marathon running, food, and people I have never heard of.

The verbal seas part when Handbag Lady speaks. She is thinking of expanding to belts and eyeglasses and becoming a spokeswoman for a charity although she is not sure which one. The only nonrunner guest is a plus-size model presently studying elocution. She really wants to get into commercials. Her husband recently purchased an airplane. He is thinking of trying a new career. And then the talk turns to children. Harris and I become quiet. Schools and croup are not our world. And further, this is a subject we have not broached. It is too soon, I tell myself. But I experience an ache as our guests talk Dalton, Nightingale, Collegiate, and other private New York City schools whose individual tuitions could be the salvation for a small South American country.

Everyone seems to like the pie. I take a beat to relax. The end of my audition is nearing.

"Maria, you really should have the coffee made," barks Harris at our chance encounter in the kitchen. "You bought ice cream, right?"

"Yes, vanilla," I say calmly, but I am reaching my girlfriend limit. I scan my brain for the universal back-off gesture as I fantasize about emptying the entire half gallon on his head.

And then they are all calling it a night and heading out into the clean cold Hamptons air and I am so relieved I almost cry.

"The chicken was good," Harris says. I smile, but I am sort of feeling like I don't care. "Is the kitchen cleaned up?"

"All clean," I say, pulling off my clothes in preparation for sleep. We lie in bed silently. It begins to occur to me that I don't know Harris. Then I think I may and there just isn't much to know, but that contravenes all of my assumptions. For me everyone is complex, filled with secrets waiting to be discovered.

FEBRUARY 11 "We went to the country," I say to Jed Monday morning, just for practice. I baked chickens, cleaned house, and drove around doing errands. Now I am back in the city at work. So, this is what it is like to be normal. I look up at Jed. "Hey, you don't look so good," I say.

Jed removes his phone headset, comes out of his cubicle, and ushers me into my office. He shuts the door behind him. Never a good sign in the agency business.

"Barry Hovington is missing," Jed grimly states.

"What do you mean?" I ask, not yet even trying to process this information.

Jed does a long shallow exhalation. "I mean, he didn't get on the flight from London to L.A." Then another shorter exhalation. "His wife called to say she hasn't seen him for days, and apparently no one has."

"Frankly, I think he has a girlfriend in Provence," I say. "And so far he has only missed one flight, right?"

Jed tries to respond. “Well, ah . . .”

I cut him off. “So let’s not get crazy here, okay?” I beg. I am probably right, Barry is probably fine, but images of the sitcom writer who was found seated in his car in a parking garage only after rigor mortis had set in comes to mind. “I need Barry to sell that pitch. We have got to find him, and get him on a plane to L.A. today,” I emphatically intone.

“More like yesterday,” Jed says.

“Okay, first reschedule all of his meetings that were for today,” I instruct offhandedly, as if I don’t know getting people together in a room in L.A. is a small miracle. No one does anything there, but everyone is really busy. “I’ll work on tracking down Barry,” I confidently continue. Jed is already back at his station leaving word for assistants who are not yet in on the West Coast. I am seated at my desk feigning a meditative state trying to channel Barry. My agency contract hangs by a thread. My one A-list client is lost.

I’ve always wanted to travel to Europe without luggage and now I am. Too many hours with no Barry. I hand my boarding pass to the flight attendant just as she is meant to close the door. I will drag him to Los Angeles to pitch his one line, dead or alive. At this moment I am sure I don’t care. And then we are landing.

“Why did you let me do this?” I bellow into my cell. I am exhausted and rumpled, with no idea of how even to begin to look for the missing Barry. “Jed?” I say into the little phone, fearful of having lost my lifeline.

“He’s found,” says Jed.

“Where?” I ask.

"He's at American waiting for the next flight to Los Angeles. You're booked on the flight also."

"He's here in Heathrow?" I ask, trying to get my bearings.

"It's a thing," Jed explains.

"How do you know?" I ask. In the film business certain latitude is given for idiosyncratic behavior. Allowances are made until they are not. Barry Hovington is always late. Since everyone knows this, it must be factored into all of Barry's scheduling. As the agent, I should have known.

"Hey, Barry," I say as I sidle up to him in the First Class lounge.

"You look like shit, old gal," he replies. I do not respond. I am mad, but grateful. Mortality is part of show business too. Barry smiles. He now knows how far I'll go.

The seats in First Class are so much nicer. I've been bumped up so I can sit with Barry. I am the Brinks guard and he is the loot. Max Rubin, a pretty big producer, is seated behind us. I must wait until we reach cruising altitude to assess the rest of the First Class cargo. So far Barry has limited his intake to pure orange juice. I am poised to store my anxiety in the overhead bin. I fold myself into the big leather seat and think of Harris. Life could still work out.

There is someone pounding on the bathroom door. What about the OCCUPIED sign? I hurry to exit this hateful little chamber. As I open the door Max Rubin slams his body up against mine. He pushes me back into the airplane head with force.

"Take the pitch off the market until I see if I can finance it," he demands.

"Make me a firm offer," I shoot back as I stare into his nasal passage.

"Take it off the fuckin' market," he barks.

"Technically it's not on the market yet, Max," I inform him with all of the aplomb I can muster stuffed into the First Class pisser of American flight #103.

"Listen, you little bitch, I want the next J. C. Izod film, and I don't want to get into a fucking bidding war," says Max. He is pressing my back up against the sink and it hurts. Why do men in Hollywood wear black T-shirts with navy blazers?

I think of changing the subject to Max's sartorial faux pas, but instead snap back with, "A million bucks takes it off the table."

"You little cunt, I haven't even heard the entire pitch yet," he says.

Oh, yes, you have, Max, I think to myself. A naked man runs across the city. I rest my case. Apparently Barry has pitched Max during the thirty seconds I took for myself to go to the friggin' bathroom.

"Think about it, would ya?" Max pleads.

I stare into the middle distance, trying to calculate if my desire to urinate is outweighed by my desire to get away from the rabid producer. Someone else is pounding on the bathroom door. "We're full up," I scream out.

"What are you two doing in there?" cries Barry with a wicked laugh.

"Just chatting," I cry as Max liberates me and the bathroom door flies open.

FEBRUARY 12 My homeland, land of the unflattering light. No wonder everyone here gets plastic surgery. I drop Barry at what appears to be the Leave It to Beaver Hotel, his friend's private Beverly Hills estate, and instruct the driver to head over the hill to my mother's. I feel a gentle wave of relief as the car pulls up to the welcoming two-story house with the shiny black door. I put the key—the same one I've had since the sixth grade—into the lock, and I am almost back to the beginning.

"Hey Ma," I say rushing toward my mother who is in the living room seated at her nineteenth-century desk.

"How's it going at R. J. Reynolds?" she asks, demonstrating no surprise at my arrival.

"Ma, R. J. Reynolds is a tobacco company. I work at a talent agency," I explain for the nine millionth time.

"Oh well," she says, continuing her paper work. "Frankly, I don't know what it is you do. Are you staying long?"

"No, I am leaving in a few hours. May I borrow some clothes?"

"Sure. At this point everything I own is vintage," she says. "Take your pick. And call your brother and say hello, will you?"

"I'll try," I say as I head for her closet. I settle for a Diane von Furstenberg wraparound shirtdress and a pair of Evans high heels.

Too much of a fashion statement, I think as we teeter into the agency, me in my heels, and Barry in his cups. Crocodile Boy meets us in the foyer. He is primed to become Barry's "West Coast representative." He is an eager young agent ready to snap up the clients of others, not quite yet himself a signer. Crocodile Boy is on and Barry is lapping it up. He just loves Barry's films, his writing, his directing, his brilliant use of . . .

I am the invisible girl. The men are talking not over me, not around me, but through me. I have ceased to exist. I hate Crocodile Boy. A mean little phony with yellow teeth and an Armani suit he bought on layaway. A sycophant of a person standing on his tippy top toes. Dancing at the end of a yardarm, looking forward to wealth and power and a life of bending over to get it. "Don't mind me, you talented rogue," he cries as he folds himself over.

"Gee, that's great," I say at regular intervals, nodding submissively as the two men swagger. Furtively looking at my watch as we make the rounds. Have we not bonded enough?

"Okay, so you have the rent-a-car. You know where you are going. We will stay in constant communication," I instruct as we sit in the Polo Lounge. Barry is wired. He feels it. He's got something the town wants. And he is wearing it like a new dress. I just pray I can keep the pressure on, and that no one realizes the paucity of what it is they desire. The priceless sentence. "You will show up at all of the meetings, right?" I question/command, counting on the fact that he has already done his compulsory no-show by missing his original flight and the first day of scheduled meetings. "You can call me at any time of the day or night," I say, wishing I hadn't, wanting to kill myself because I have.

"No problem, ole gal," he says as I exit into an airport-bound car. As the driver pulls away I peer out the back window and stare at Barry standing at the entrance of the Beverly Hills Hotel. I try not to worry.

I am so tired I literally don't know what day it is. I have upgraded myself to First Class. I am chugging champagne and looking forward to sleep, and to New York City, and to my three thousand miles of buffer from all that ails me.

FEBRUARY 16 Wyatt James is frantic. She hopped right over the tracks to great wealth when she married Martin, the founder of an important hedge fund. She is an attractive tall-and-lanky with sandy long hair and a pinched expression that connotes her belief that some bureaucratic arm, of which she is specifically unaware, will find her out and take it all back. She spends with enormous gusto and collects people to fill in as guests at the tables she purchases at all of the most important charity functions in New York.

"Harris, Maria, how great to see you," she greets us in the hallowed halls of Chelsea Piers. Harris beams. He has never met Wyatt, but is pleased to be recognized. These are my people. To them I am a minor party favor. A single girl who has something to do with the movies and can hold her own during dinner. And, too, Wyatt cares. She wishes I would find "Him," and have a family before it is too late. So she embraces Harris, a TV something, who adds to her table and is a potential mate for a smaller player for whom she has a certain fondness. All minor players move on, Wyatt says with a glance. These are the rules as we play them. But Harris's feet seem to be stuck in cement. He wants more. I nudge his gaze, first, toward a movie star in the crowd—the telephone caller from Bingham's office; star gazer, meet star pervert—and then toward a well-known model. And suddenly he moves. Everything he wants is in this room. I turn and he is gone into the sea of the rich and famous.

Once dinner is served Harris returns. He is seated between an unattractive heiress and a beautiful South American wife. My dinner companions are a U.S. senator and the billionaire husband of the South American. We talk movies and money, Bermuda and national security. I concentrate on shrinking just enough so the men can talk, but not so much that they can't avoid one another.

In my champagne haze I enter the dance floor with Wyatt's husband, Martin. He curls and whirls and dips me around. I think I feel his hand wend its way up my little black dress. And so, I keep dancing, no response to his offer, no bargain to play. We understand one another. He dips me again and lets me go with a smile.

I am at once confronted by the billionaire. "What do you think of your boyfriend and my wife going off to Chamonix to ski?" he inquires.

"He's very trustworthy," I respond quickly with confidence. I file this away. No matter what Harris is up to, I cannot care. There is no time to find another Harris or concern myself with stupid men tricks. I have Barry Hovington driving around Los Angeles in a convertible and probably three fertile eggs tops. To say that I have no leverage is an understatement. All systems here are go. Let Harris and the beautiful South American climb up a mountain in France and ski down. There is so little time before the bell rings and I am officially deemed old and unattractive; considerations such as these have little meaning to me.

"I may go skiing with Alonzia," Harris reports as he piles into bed.

"Oh," I say, trying for impartiality. We are in his bed. These are his terms.

"She's a first-class athlete; we really get along." He smiles, clearly pleased with himself. "She's even luged," he says dreamily as he leans over and extinguishes the lights.

Harris pulls me toward him, a rarity at night. He is a morning man. Sex is required between 6:00 and 7:15 A.M., after sleep and before running. But he wants it now, as he basks in social victory. His fit arms and small torso feel good as he presses up against me. He kisses me softly. We settle into a gentle rhythm, and I allow my perceptions to recede.

My brain tells me I should get out of bed. After the first two weeks birth control has become my responsibility. Most mornings I get up before him to ready myself. There are these thoughts, and then the gentle movement gives way to something more important and steady. And then I give in, and there is no more thinking, just feeling, then sleep.

FEBRUARY 18 "You don't think you are going to sell that piece of shit sentence, do you?" cackles Crocodile Boy over the phone. So much for the West Coast team.

"I've got another call," I say and jump to . . .

"I've been driving round this fucking hellhole for days. Hasn't anyone made an offer yet?" screams Barry into the ear still ringing with Crocodile's cackle.

"Barry, where are you?" I ask, stalling for time to think of something to say.

"On my way to a fucking watering hole. This is a desert out here."

"Hold tight," I say. "It's always like this. The calm before the storm." I am silently praying for a miracle.

"Like fucking hell," he screams, and cuts out or hangs up. Who really knows with cell phones anyway?

The phone rings again. Maybe he didn't hang up. "Hello," I say into the receiver.

"Is Jed there?" a young voice questions.

"This is his assistant," I reply.

"Cool," says the voice on the other end of the line. "What can you tell me about the J. C. Izod pitch?"

"Who wants to know?" I ask back.

"Oh, it's Julie," she says.

Whatever. I take a deep breath, prepared to give fate a proper nudge. "Well, J. C. is very hot for the project. His studio just made a firm offer."

"Oh, gawd," she says in Southern Californian. "You mean, like, the studio where he has his overall? Or, like, the studio that produced his latest film?"

"Both," I say and hang up before I am required to elaborate.

"Who the hell is Julie?" I scream out into the hallway.

Jed peers up at me from his station through cloudy glasses and shrugs. "I dunno," he says.

"Some young girl just called to ask about the pitch," I say. Still staring. Wanting answers.

"It happens all day long—they're Trackers," Jed explains. People paid by producers to track information.

"What do you tell them?" I ask in an accusatory tone.

"Depends," he says.

"On what?" I ask as I feel my blood rising.

"My mood." He smiles.

Hollywood runs on levels of lies. "Well, I just told her we have two firm offers," I admit so that our two levels can keep the story straight.

"Good." He smiles knowingly.

Bingham walks into my office and closes the door. She is smoking, definitely an infraction.

"I am fired," she says.

"I am next," I say, feeling the fear.

"I am going on holiday and then opening my own shop," she informs. More dissemination of false information.

"Good for you," I say, wondering if her little holiday might not be to rehab.

"Good luck," she says, mustering all of the bravado she possibly can to make it to the door.

"You, too," I say, feeling myself falling from the nineteenth floor. I flash on my irresponsible sex of the preceding night. A thought I have managed to hide in a box in my brain for most of the day. I flash on myself homeless and pregnant.

"Max Rubin, on line one," yells Jed.

"Hello," I say into the receiver with as much machismo as I can muster.

"You have offers?" he asks.

I breathe into the phone, trying to focus.

"Don't start, Maria," he says, barely holding it together.

"What do you want, Max?" I ask.

"Listen, you fucking . . ." He stops himself.

"The client wants a million bucks," I say. I am winning. I have not demonstrated my desperation, nor have I lied.

"You're outta your mind," he says. I remain silent. "I'll call you back," he says.

"Let's clear out," I say to Jed. It is 5:45 P.M.

His expression displays shock. "It's only 2:45 in L.A.," he feels compelled to remind me.

"Forward my calls to my cell," I demand. "If we stay here nothing is sure to happen."

We wait for The Radical Theatre Agent, briefcase in hand,

to pass by. "Good night, all," his voice echoes down the hallway.

"Night," Jed and I say in unison, waiting until our superior officer is clearly out of sight to make our move.

I walk up Sixth Avenue to Central Park South and head west. I am doing it. I am almost living the life I have always wanted. I am in love or close enough to be heading to Citarella to buy lamb chops to broil for Harris and myself up at my place. I walk fast, keeping up with the stream of pedestrian traffic crossing at Columbus Circle. I look smart. I am wearing simple gabardine slacks, a cashmere sweater set, Chanel flats, and an Armani jacket. My hair is smoothed back into a ponytail. I am carrying a canvas L. L. Bean bag for my scripts and groceries. I am a New Yorker. I have made it. I want to lick the sidewalks to prove how much it means to me. Look at me. I am going to make it across the finish line, just in time. Just before the clock strikes.

My cell phone starts its incessant cry. I move out of the fast-moving pedestrian lane and switch it on.

"Take the pitch off the market and I'll get you $750,000," Max screams.

"Hey, Max," I say.

"Quit stalling, Maria," he says. "Let's go," he demands.

I am making this dinner. I keep walking toward Broadway. I will not let this interrupt my dinner. "Max, there is no one else at this moment. Make me an offer I can take to my client," I say.

"Take it off the market," he screams.

"It's off," I say, annoyed.

"Okay, I am offering you $750,000 for the pitch. I just need to clear it with my financiers," he continues.

"What does that mean?" I say.

"Give me an hour," he says.

"Good luck," I say as I continue my journey to the meat market.

I stand outside Citarella on Broadway and West Seventy-fifth Street dialing for dollars. "Would you take $750,000?" I ask Barry.

"I had my heart set on a million," he whines. "Can't you get me a million?" he stammers.

"I'll try," I say.

I call Jed. "Let's start dialing," I say. We both race into action disseminating the information that we are poised. The bidding seems to be starting around $800,000.

I pick out roasting potatoes, haricots verts, some nice butter lettuce, tomatoes, all beautiful and overpriced, to go with the most expensive lamb chops known to man, and head up toward West Eighty-first and Central Park West. En route I stop at a bakery and buy a chocolate custard cake. I know this is my moment and I mean to celebrate.

I have never been as happy as I am slathering these chops with overpriced olive oil, rosemary, and garlic. If I sell the pitch then . . . Freddie buzzes from downstairs.

"Mr. Schwartzman is here," he announces.

"Send him up," I reply. I can't wait to see Harris.

"You do have a great view," he announces, looking out at the planetarium, the park, and the city beyond.

"I love the juxtaposition of the Chrysler building and the AT&T building," I say with a little too much college art history in tow.

He pulls me toward him. "You smell good," he remarks.

"I am excited about a potential sale," I proudly announce.

"Did you buy any bread?" he asks. I happily pull a baguette out of a bag on the counter of the teeny kitchen. His face falls. "I don't like that kind," he says.

"What if we doctor it up, and make it into garlic bread?" I try.

"Okay," he says, responding like a petulant child. He walks off in search of the television clicker and sports and news, and news and sports and news, *click, click, click* . . .

I watch Harris lustily gnaw away at his third chop. His posture remains erect. He reminds me of an aggressive kid in the third grade. He always knows the answer. He is always right. I know you know the answer, I want to say as I smile at him and he smiles back with olive oil and lamb juice smeared across his face.

My cell phone starts its incessant ringing. I rush into the little kitchen where I have left it. "It's well over an hour," I start in.

"What?" the voice on the other end of the line questions.

"Who is this?" I demand. "It's J. C.," the voice answers back.

Movie stars don't call other people's agents; their people do. "Yes?" I say with bravado.

"I want to do the Naked Movie. Don't do anything until my producing partner calls you," he demands. Then in a more plaintive voice, "Can you wait until tomorrow?" If this is Jed or one of his friends they are good. It sounds like J. C. Izod.

"Sure, I am in the middle of something right now anyway," I respond with a hint of devil-may-care.

"Great. If you don't hear from him, call me," he says and then gives me an L.A. number. "Did you get that?" he asks.

"I wrote it down," I say, not believing this entire conversation.

"Great," he says, and then he is gone.

"I think J. C. Izod may have just called," I shout out to Harris. I am so close. And then the phone rings again. It is probably the prankster revealing his identity. Okay, so I am not so close. "Hello," I say, resigned.

"Give me till tomorrow morning," Max barks.

"Make me an offer tomorrow," I say. Max hangs up. Oh, my God, there could be a bidding war.

I serve Harris the chocolate custard cake. He is subdued. I hope it is just the result of too much food. He leans back in the rickety wooden country French chair that goes with the dining room table. He seems to be assessing me. I want him to love me so badly it hurts. But what can I do?

"Did I ever tell you about my relationship with Pari Reid?" he asks.

"The movie star?" I ask.

"Yes." He nods brashly. I believe him. I happen to know a few short, far less attractive producer types that Pari pursued. She must have a thing for short TV producers.

"She sublet my Paris apartment when I was off working freelance," he begins. He is sitting very upright in his chair. He is proud. Movie stars may talk to me in my kitchen, but he has nailed one in his Paris apartment. "I had a project with the BBC. We were shooting in Africa," he continues. I may be contemplating the sale of one-line pitches to the movies for seven figures, but he has filmed in friggin' Africa. "So she's living in my apartment. And when my friends call she's inviting them over for drinks, and little dinner parties. And she is writing me notes accompanied by the rent checks informing me of all of this." He's on autopilot. He's told this story so many times it is worn. "And then she sends me pictures of herself wearing my clothes," he says with all of his male pride openly exposed, the slight perversity of the images tingling his tongue.

"Wow," I say, doing my best to hang on his every word. There is a small knot forming in the pit of my stomach. I may play a man at the office, but technically I am a girl. I continue to nod in feigned appreciation of all of the painful detail.

"Well, we agree to meet in Morocco," he continues, "where she meets me in a limousine, and, well, we do it right there parked at the curb after she sends the driver off on some impossible errand."

Harris laughs. He is all puffed up. Take that for trying to earn a living in the boys' arena. I feel ill. I plaster on a smile and begin to clear the dinner dishes.

"Wow," I say with my back to him, heading toward the kitchen sink. I taste the salt from two hot tears that have found their way all the way to my mouth.

Again we make love at night. At first I imagine he is thinking of Pari Reid, but as his amazing kisses continue all thoughts ebb. I cannot remember ever feeling such a perfect fit. When we are together there is nothing else—just soft caressing waves of pleasure and delight. Again I am unprepared. He is breathing loudly, embraced by sleep. I lie awake knowing what I think I want. I have to tell him what I want. The only honest agent. I get up and go to the bathroom.

I finger a package of four birth control pills I have obtained from my gynecologist, Martin Drink. "You're nearing the end of the game," he said. If you think you ever want to get pregnant, don't take these." I know I want to get pregnant. I also know I am tricking Harris. "If you take four of these pills within forty-eight hours even if you fertilize an egg, it won't be able to implant,"

Dr. Drink explained. “Don’t take ’em,” he reiterated. I put the package back in the medicine chest and head back to bed. I try to make my breathing coincide with that of Harris’s, and then I sleep.

FEBRUARY 20 "I am going to quit and grow pasta plants for a living," I say.

"Okay, I am going to run to Colorado. I'll be right back," Jed responds.

We are suffering from cabin fever. It has been two days since J. C. Izod called, and neither he nor Max nor absolutely anybody has called. No offers.

"Do you think they are trying to smoke us out?" I ask, and then Jed and I laugh uncontrollably. I imagine Barry driving round and round in tight little circles in his rent-a-convertible in a deserted L.A. parking lot. Jed stares at me as if he has lost all belief. I start singing *"There's no business like show business,"* just to keep the troops mobilized.

And then Jed calls out. "Max Rubin on line one."

"Hello," I say.

"Seven fifty," he says.

"Is this a firm offer?" I ask.

"Yep."

"I have to talk to my client," I say.

"I'll hold."

Jed, who has been listening on the other phone, signals that he is attempting to locate Barry. "Barry on line two," he shouts out.

"Max Rubin is offering you $750,000," I say.

"So low?" screams Barry. For less than ten words it ain't bad. And then it is as if I am being dragged by a speeding car as I hold on to a frayed rope. Barry is doing a British sputtering thing.

"Take a deep breath," I instruct. "I'll tell him you need to think it over."

"Max, he needs to think it over," I say.

"Quickly," Max shouts. "I need to know today!" he barks, and then he slams down the phone.

"I left my old Bozos because you fucking said you could fucking well do the job," Barry screams.

"Right," I say. "I'll get to it."

I quickly call all of the players who have expressed interest, including J. C. Izod's phone machine, and say I have a firm offer. And then the phone starts ringing, and men start screaming.

First I am getting my client a million bucks for nothing. Then I am bilking a major studio out of a million five. Then a million seven. Then Max calls wanting an answer, and threatening to sue. No time for legal theories. The phone keeps ringing. Then Crocodile Boy calls.

"What's fucking happening?" he shouts at the top of his little lungs. "Tell me everything. I need to know. I always knew this would sell."

Then Max calls again. "I want an answer now!" he screams.

And then Barry: "I want more," he yells.

And then La Studio Head, the female voice of reason: "We would like to take the pitch off the table for two," she says. "The offer will terminate at the conclusion of this telephone conversation," she politely adds.

"Sold," I say.

"Fine, I will have business affairs call you immediately to initiate the paperwork."

I have just sold seven words for two million dollars.

"Barry, we've just accepted two million," I say.

"Can't you get it any higher?" he asks.

I walk out of the office into the chilly spring air wanting to forget everything, knowing I have to meet Harris at a cocktail party of some of his people. I promise myself not to mention anything about the sale. If movie stars' calls lead to stories of limousine sex I don't want to know what news of a two-million-dollar sale might do.

I am feeling hollow. Harris was so excited to have secured an invitation to this musty midtown town house he could barely contain himself. We have arranged to meet here. I stand in the crowd searching for him. Finber, the little Irishman from dinner party number one, sees me and makes his way over.

"Hello," he says in a big friendly manner.

"Hello," I say, wanting to get away.

An attractive bouncy girl sidles up. "Hey," she says, while simultaneously waving at close range.

"Hey," we say back to get it to stop.

"One of Harris's exes," Fin feels the need to share as she bounces off. He searches for my reaction. He smiles. I smile back. "She's an actress. She and Harris dated 'bout seven months, then one day she just walks into his apartment and takes her stuff. And it's over," the little Irishman reports with glee. Am I doing something wrong here? "He really only liked her for her car." That hurt. I stand silently, refusing to react. "No need to tell Harris I told you 'bout that," he adds. I nod and move away.

Here I am again in the midst of the attractive well-educated set. The good memorizers. They are really really motivated, but not quite where they want to be. I wonder if they will ever be. Harvard may have been the apogee, you guys, but keep trying, you never know. I search for Harris, no luck. Change rooms, more mustiness, no Harris. And finally I see him. Harris gazing up at a man twice his size, a Pew or a Dupont, or perhaps a Rockefeller, something, but definitely not a Kennedy. From this vantage point I realize that Harris is one of those people who stands too close.

I think of just leaving and then I see that Harris is aware of my presence. Without shifting his gaze of adoration he is trying to motion me to his side. He moves his chin in a ticlike manner. He cups and flaps the hand connected to the arm at his side (the non-champagne-holding one) in the subtle universal gesture of *Come here now*. I have just suffered hours of unrelenting male aggression and now I am meant to heel, point, and not bark.

"This is Maria O'Mara," Harris says in his most obsequious tone.

"Nice to see you," I say, offering my hand. Mr. Social Register accepts my hand and adds a disinterested nod demonstrating his social grace.

"Is it related to the woodcock?" Harris asks.

"Different family," Mr. Social Register answers.

Mr. Social Register stands powerless as Harris continues his interrogation regarding the double-breasted something, not a blazer, but a bird. Harris is angling for something. The Blue Blood is retreating. Harris persists. Finally, I can't stand it any longer. Still having not ascertained what Harris is after, I meander over to the bar, bad dog that I am.

Just when I think I am safe old Finber corners me. "Pretty fine drinks here, eh?" he starts in again.

I smile and nod and inch back. What is it with these people? They all stand too close.

"You know, even if Harris does wangle an invitation to Maine ya won't be getting one of the good rooms," he informs me. One mystery solved. "We're pretty fed up with him always takin' the best room for himself in this group. We will all be standin' around not wantin' to take it, and then he just grabs for it. Takes the key to the best room. All for himself, like he's entitled or somethin'."

I wonder if you get a certificate to establish membership in "The Group." I'd love to stay and see if Harris is able to secure an invitation to Maine or if Fin will be able to maintain without passing out, but alas my public calls. I inch my way along an interior wall away from the ranting Fin, through the throngs of social hopefuls, and out into the cold.

The wind feels great blowing up my pleated Prada. I ache from the general New York buzz that grabs at you with the first waking horn or tire screech, from greedy white men who yell from three thousand miles away, and from social-climbing, *Vanity Fair*–reading, Beaujolais Nouveau–sipping lovers who just want to be invited. I walk west on Fiftieth Street and turn onto Madison. I look up at Villard House and decide to take myself to a celebratory dinner for one at Le Cirque.

"One please," I say.

"Does Madame have a reservation?" the worried maitre d' asks.

Usually I am good at restaurants. Am I losing my edge?

"No, this is an impromptu celebration," I confidently explain.

Mauro, the son of the owner, flashes me a smile. I am immediately shown to a table.

I luxuriate in the plush green booth. It is good to be alive.

"Try this wine," Mauro suggests, and he hands me a glass.

"So you did well today, eh?" his father, Sirio, comments.

And for the first time I let myself enjoy my small victory. The Maccionis reward me with fabulous dishes all perfectly choreographed toward warmth and satisfaction. "Brava, bella," they say as I get up to leave. And then there in my path is Pari Reid.

"I think I am one of your agents," I say. "And if I am not I should be."

She smiles. "Who ya with?" she good-naturedly demands.

I flash my card.

"Left you guys this morning," she exclaims.

"I am sorry to hear that," I say. "Perhaps you'll come back."

She smiles her movie star smile. And then I just can't help myself.

"We have some friends in common," I say.

"Oh, who?" she politely inquires.

"Let's just say they're short and dark and call themselves producers," I say.

"Oh, well then we're related." She laughs and locks pinkies with me before heading off to the loo.

I step off the curb into an awaiting cab. We swoosh up Madison, cross at Seventy-ninth Street, zip through the park, and I am home. When I enter my apartment the phone is ringing. And then it stops, and the hang-up sound echoes through the living room. I make my way to the bathroom and the package of four birth control pills. I swig down all four and head for bed.

FEBRUARY 21 The Radical Theatre Agent slaps a copy of the trades onto my desk. There on the front page is a picture of Crocodile Boy slapping Barry Hovington on the back. The lead story in both publications is Crocodile Boy's big sale. "He got to the press first," says The Radical Theatre Agent with disappointment. I feel my soul belly-flop against the printed page. The Radical Theatre Agent breathes into my face. His have-I-taught-you-nothing glare penetrates. "I thought we weren't supposed to talk to the press," I snap back, sounding like a wounded girl.

"We lied," he laughs. "Your name is in there plenty of times. He covered his ass and got the glory," he adds as he dashes off to ruin someone else's day. He stole the glory.

I feel the underpinnings of my well-structured life ripping apart. There is a metal-hitting-metal sound, and then a wave of fatigue. A girl fighter pilot has been hit. I wait to assess the severity of the damage. Jed smiles weakly, searching for the right words. He is saying something to me, but I can't hear. There is just the loud grinding sound. And too much disappointment. And then I remember I have promised to meet Harris for a late lunch.

I have not seen or talked to Harris directly since my disappearing act last night. It is one of those my-person-called-your-person arranged lunches. If only assistants could arrange marriages.

"You can't just leave like that," he admonishes me. He is impaling mashed potatoes. I guess last night wasn't a deal breaker if he feels the need to continue to teach me how to behave. But as I stare at him across the table and he continues to mutter on about comportment and friends and other such matters (which I happen to believe he knows very little about) I wonder what it is he is really talking about. I hope he has remembered to wash off the residue of reality programming as I watch him lustily devour the fried chicken he has ordered.

"The skiing trip to Chamonix has been called off," he remarks, seeming both surprised and disappointed. I keep wiping my own face in the hopes that he will realize he has fried chicken crust on his, but he remains oblivious.

"That's a shock," I say, envisioning the seething billionaire on the dance floor.

"What do you mean? Alonzia really wanted to go. It was a scheduling snafu," he explains. Insensitivity as art. "Anyway, because I am not going I think we should plan something together." He leans forward and puts my hand in his. "Let's try," he says.

The warmth of his hand is too much. Big embarrassing tears begin to spill.

"Maria, what is it?" he says, truly baffled.

"I am just having a really bad day," I say.

"Did someone say something to you at the party last night?" he questions.

Harris isn't such a bad old guy. I look down at my croque-monsieur and attempt to gather myself.

"We'll go out to Water Mill and plant bulbs," he says.

I nod in agreement. And at that moment something is different. One switch has gone off and another seems to have been ignited. I can physically feel the fight receding. I have worked so hard to get here. The thought that I might just let it all go like a big white balloon astounds me. And yet I feel my attention turning toward soil deposits, shingling roofs, and proper roasting pans more easily than I could have ever imagined. I am not sure if it is an excuse for my own mediocrity or a realization of what it is that I really want.

"Crocodile Boy on line one," Jed calls out.

"I don't know how those things got in the press," he launches.

"Yeah, I wonder," I say. I am on dangerous ground. I am not being politic and everyone knows that Crocodile Boy is a favorite of the Grand Poo Bah.

"I don't think you're being fair, and I don't like your attitude," Crocodile whines.

"Frankly my dear . . . ," I say, giving it my best Clark Gable. I hang up.

"Barry on line two," Jed announces.

"You know, Crocodile told me if you had kept him in the loop we would have gotten double," he complains.

"No doubt," I say. "Jed and I will stay here tonight and get the deal with the studio hammered out."

"When do you think my first payment will arrive, old girl?"

"Soon," I say. "Congratulations."

"Oh yes, well, you too," he says.

"Barry," I say, "perhaps you'll come and visit my boyfriend and me out in Water Mill before you head home."

"Oh, the Hamptons, *très chic*," he retorts. "I'd like that."

I am not completely finished. I must win back the affection of my A-list client. Barry and Harris in one room, a frightening thought.

MARCH 9 I am dancing out on the plains somewhere on the border of domesticity and denial. It's amazing how many different kinds of polish there are. I am standing in the Southampton Hardware Store actually studying cleaning agents. Harris and I have established a nice domestic rhythm. Since our famous "Let's Try" lunch, we now have dinner together most nights in the city even when he is shooting late. To a producer that is big. On the weekends we head out to Water Mill.

During the week mostly I shop for the food and prepare it at his place. He usually supplies the wine. We eat, chat about current events, clean up, and head for bed, where we read. If there is sports on we watch that together. And then we knit our bodies into a reassuring knot and sleep. In the morning we have what I consider superior domestic sex. By which I mean that although our moves have a ritual precision to them, they are athletic and satisfying. I love the way he feels and smells. I've accepted his peccadilloes as part of the fabric of my life.

At the moment I am just letting work pass over me in a big wave. I have made a couple of not so important deals, and I am trying to keep my head down. I am focusing on the spiritual, i.e., the fact that I paid some guy four hundred bucks to bless and clear my office, and that surely such a ritual will placate the gods and save me. It is a lot easier than hoping to sign some twenty-million-dollar a picture player, which at this point is highly unlikely and the only thing in the temporal world that is guaranteed to save my ass.

This weekend we are finally planting the bulbs and doing a spring housecleaning, thus the polish. After the hardware store I am heading to the Southampton Cheese Store. I am making Harris porcini pasta and am looking for just the right cheese to complement the meal.

It all seems fine and yet there is something subversive about so much domesticity. I am up at 5 A.M. patrolling. I keep thinking that whatever it is that is troubling me is out there in those early hours. If I capture it and know it maybe then it won't be so frightening.

MARCH 27 The midtown hustle. I make my way through the whiteness of The Radical Theatre Agent's favorite midtown haunt. I have been summoned, and I am late. A wave of anger stirs in me. Would it have been so difficult to wait for me? Another power dance, and now I am in trouble. Why do they all have to be so mean? So Armani? Waves of septic ire, and then—air kisses and lies, the signature talk of the trade.

"How fun to have you all to myself," I purr, hoping to hang on to my job.

"So you're a veteran now with a couple of major sales under your belt," he says, looking over my head to see the more important. A congratulatory lunch? I think not.

"So," he launches in, "will Barry be coming into New York before he returns to the U.K.? I would love to get to know him." And there it is in the first few minutes of conversation. Step aside, little girl, I made you and now I will break you. But what about me? I sold his lousy pitch for two big ones. I whistle into the wind. Chump change, he chugs, and besides, that was weeks ago, ancient history. The words that are not spoken blare in my ears.

Suddenly The Radical Theatre Agent is blowing kisses. He does love me. And then I follow the airstream on which the kisses are delivered to the recipient, an overweight theater diva, lapping it up. She waddles over on her way out. Her cleavage pouring, her words boring. And then she is gone.

"So who else on your list is poised for greatness?" he demands. The Radical Theatre Vulture.

"They all are," I answer back. "Or I wouldn't have signed them." Touché. We are so over. So well done.

The Radical Theatre Agent gets up and wires himself for the half-block walk. He smiles at me.

"Thank you," I begin.

"Shhh," he angrily intones. "I am on the fucking phone." He walks on ahead, lost in the wall of people who have sprouted up through the sidewalk during lunch.

I make my way to the drugstore on West Fifty-seventh Street. Down into the basement of toilet paper, Q-tips, nasal spray, and pregnancy tests. Now which one do I want? Along with the worries of no job, Harris vanishing, and nuclear war is the worry that there is a non-stress-related reason I have not had my period in almost two months. I figure it is worth eighteen bucks to ease my mind. I snap up the package from the counter and the darting eyes of the knowing cashier. May be trouble, she smiles. I search for the middle distance and glide back to the office, cross-country style. Large long loping steps to the elevator, the nineteenth floor, and my fate.

I huddle in the infamous third stall. First Bingham tying off and shooting up, now me peeing onto the little strip and then waiting for the code, not Morse, but just as powerful. I look at the little circle and the little square on the plastic pregnancy strip. Eighteen bucks for this? The markup is phenomenal. Now, if there is a line in each shape, what does that mean? I read and reread the explanation. One if by sea, two if by land? No, that's not it. Two means a little Harris. I am glad and scared and stunned. I slide the strip back in its case. Shove the news back into my purse and wonder what I will do next.

MARCH 29 I am racing up Broadway on foot ever hopeful that I will be able to catch a cab although now I am mostly there. I have a cab problem. When I am really in a hurry I cannot catch one. It is a personal failing I am willing to own and yet it continues to make me feel bad, inferior to all other New Yorkers who surely don't share this affliction. I am meeting Harris for the ballet. I have never told him I love him, and I am . . . I can't say that word, not even in my head. I am jumping on cement without bending my knees. Flat-footed smacks that vibrate through my whole body, which is now a holding tank for someone else.

We stand in the plaza above the street. The cold spry wind is whistling through the travertine halls and up my skirt exactly where my thoughts keep landing. I focus a smile on Harris and forcefully think how great he is, and his posture seems to improve. Radio signals between the two of us. He beams back and then his eyes begin to dance. The arm is up and he is frantically waving around the fountain and straight at Mr. Social Register. Still campaigning for that invitation. I want to walk over and forcefully press my hands down on Harris's shoulders as he jumps up to be recognized. See Me. Like Me. Invite Me, he flashes.

Harris starts walking toward the entrance to the State Theater, straight up to Mr. Social Register, who, it seems, is also a balletomane. They have so much in common. I stand still. I cringe at the sight of my little dark man mounted on his invisible pogo stick bouncing in circles around his social ideal. Look at me. Look at my tricks, he wails. The wounded look on the visage of Mr. Social Register pains me. Why does Harris always stand too close?

"What were you doing back there?" Harris barks as we make our way to our perfectly situated seats. "You should follow me," he scolds.

I think about that, about being a team. Am I meant to stand too close and be obsequious too? But you see, I am presently doing that for a living in Show Business. Except I refuse to stand too close. And then, as if on cue, J. C. Izod comes hopping over seats in the stately theater. He's a movie star. Rules do not apply.

"Maria," he screams in his signature comedic tones. I open my arms wide. He kisses me square on the mouth. "I am so excited about the pitch. Barry and I have been doing magnificent work out in L.A.!" he screams. His words reverberate all the way to the far balcony. People are looking. Mostly they smile. The smart ones are offended.

Harris is perched up on his toes. His gaze is expectant.

"This is my friend, Harris," I say.

"Yeah, hi," J. C. nods, polite, but curt. The lights flash. J. C. decorously crawls over a few seats to his own choice spot.

"Why didn't you say I was your boyfriend?" Harris snarls.

"Good point," I say as I grope for his hand in the dark.

MARCH 30 I wait until our morning bout. Ecstasy in unison. He is up and so out the door in his mind as I make the espresso he takes before his run. He makes it better. We both know that and still I insist. He twitches with the error of it. Bouncing on one foot and then the other. Waiting for his disappointment. I hand him the viscous mud.

"I am pregnant," I say as easily as I pass him the not so good drink.

"What?" he says. He must have misheard. There must be some mistake. I cannot bear the expression that passes across his face.

"Are you sure?" he demands. I mouth the words with him. I think this is what they must say when they are most unhappy about this particular blessing. I cannot know for sure because this is a first for me, and yet it feels right, this question and the walls crashing in simultaneously.

APRIL 1

I enter the park at Eighty-first Street en route to Dr. Drink. "P-R-E-G-N-A-N-T," I spell it out loud as I walk up the little hill near the Delacorte Theater. "Yikes," I say as someone's bike races past. "Sorry," they shout out as an afterthought. I am not sure I am.

"I took those four birth control pills you told me not to," I blurt out at Dr. Drink.

"They didn't work," he answers back. We stare at each other, wordless, pointless air. "Do you have any questions?" he asks a little harried, a little disinterested.

"What do you mean by 'high risk'?" I ask.

"You're older; we'll see if you can sustain the pregnancy. I'll call after I get the results of your blood work," he says. It is clear the dialogue is over. My time is up.

I am walking down Fifth Avenue on my way to work. Doormen, designer women, well-manicured dogs on expensive leashes, and a pregnant me.

I make my way through the day, a thin film over everyone and everything. They are speaking through water, all of these people in search of fame and fortune waiting for me to deliver.

"I think *Pussy* can be an important miniseries," my staunch angular client insists.

"I am sorry, I can't do any more body parts today," I say abruptly.

"I hope you're in heavy therapy," she retorts.

"I am in Beyond Therapy. Have you heard of it?" I ask.

"No, but I hope it works quickly," she says through gritted teeth.

"I am going out," I announce to Jed.

"Okay," he says, relieved.

I am walking through Manhattan in an unthinking state. I walk past the Flatiron Building. And then I am in a movie theater near ABC Carpet. What is this movie about anyway?

And then I walk the fifty blocks back up to my apartment. No calls from Harris on the answering machine. I wonder if he has vanished, or, worse, if he ever existed.

APRIL 3 I am inside the fishbowl looking out. Tavern on the Green definitely looked better in the coffee commercial. We have done an Art Film, and now The Reception. My colleagues are attending a theater benefit, and so coverage of this function fell to me. When an agent doesn't know anyone at the party she can always make herself useful by introducing two famous people. The famous people never notice the introducer. And anyone who does by chance happen on to the introduction naturally assumes the agent knows the people she is introducing. Show Business is so much about perception. And should be so easy. Now, if I could just find someone to introduce.

No one famous in this crowd, unless you count that old character actress who shows up at every function—she must do three or four events a night. Good makeup, though. I continue to patrol. I am beating my beat. Okay, all you filmmakers, let's get up on the dance floor and do the conga. I roam the hallowed halls of the Tavern, room after room, fat head after fat hair. As I turn one of the unending corners onto another carpeted fairway there are Harris and Fin.

They are all smiles. Chatting up the fourth runner-up in the Miss I Do Love New York contest. The girl looks down at them from her mount. I glide over and stand in their line of vision long enough to make an impression.

"Hello, you guys," I say to my two golden retrievers, caught but wagging their tails. Men can never resist a big hello. I am delighted to see Harris. It's been three days.

The situation is too dire to demonstrate displeasure. I extend my hand to the bubbling blonde.

"Maria O'Mara; nice to see you," I say.

"Hi," she speaks/whispers in her sultry tone.

Harris and I head up Central Park West on foot to my place. He puts his arm around me and holds me tightly. The air is clear and brisk.

"I have been missing you," I say.

"Me too," he says.

And then there are no more words, just each other and the big old apartment buildings that line our route and then The Museum of Natural History, and then home, and holding on as best we can.

APRIL 15 I am seated in my office busily rearranging the furniture of my mind. I have presently reached the stage where all of the furniture has been moved to the center of the room. So now what?

"Soon they'll be asking me not to attend fire drills," I say to Jed as everyone else in our row of offices races off to greet a new client, an overweight sitcom star who pulls down several million a year.

"She is lucky to have us," Jed and I say in unison, parroting The Grand Poo Bah Agent, who says that when referring to any client of the agency.

At the moment I do not exist. No one wants to tell me that my contract is not being renewed just in case I engage in some moneymaking activity, but the signs are all clear. I am uninvited to every group activity. No senior agent will make eye contact with me. And The Radical Theatre Agent keeps checking to see if every client I have has signed contract papers with the agency.

And I have no plan. It seems I am having a child and no job and Harris remains a question. He's undeclared regarding the entire situation. I am mostly living in a state of denial until I am hit with a reality flash. FLASH: You're almost jobless. FLASH: You don't have a plan. FLASH: Harris doesn't love you.

"Line two," Jed calls out just for spite. I don't bother to take the bait by asking who it is.

"Hello," I say to the mystery caller. An angry documentarian is on the phone to me. He is perplexed that a major studio won't put up millions of dollars for him to direct a mainstream comedy, something he has never done.

"They're assholes," he repeats for the ninth time at a volume nine times greater than the one at which we started.

"Uh-huh," I say, wondering why I too am not somebody else, and why somebody, anybody, won't listen to my list of complaints. Ah, the unwritten scenarios. As he persists I review my own woes. Still no declaration from Harris on the issues of anything but theater tickets and cocktail parties. Okay, we've got that. The Angry Documentarian drones on. I ruminate about what I'll do to survive should grown-up Harris walk off to a string of cocktail parties to which he couldn't possibly invite Baby Harris or me. The man has his priorities. It wasn't supposed to be like this. I take a deep breath.

"Quit sighing. You're making me nervous," complains The Angry Documentarian.

"Sorry," I say. And then he continues verbally eviscerating "those studio assholes." And I initiate Plan B. I will fly back to Los Angeles in search of a new agency.

APRIL 23 It is important to remember you can never circumvent the rules. This means you, Maria O'Mara. My string of show business meetings is not going well. And why? Well, for one thing I made all of these meetings for myself. In Hollywood somebody always calls on your behalf. I mean, even if it is a meeting with your own friggin' mother you have somebody call her and remind her how great you are. And more importantly, you remind her of all of the important people that you know. Why should your own mother or anyone else in Hollywood bother to talk to you and mean it if you can't get to the power?

I suck it up and head into the next office. I'll wow him with my confidence and wit. That ought to work.

As I enter the office I walk smack into Rich Agent Boy in midswing. "Practicing?" I say cheerfully, adroitly dodging getting whacked by his wedge.

This guy has it all. He's in his early thirties. He has an equity interest in one of the major agencies, a super rich young wife, and three adorable little kids.

"My short game is killing me," he says as he hurls a plastic whiffle ball into the plate-glass window of his corner office floating somewhere high above Wilshire Boulevard.

"Golf is very Zen," I say.

"I am not religious," he answers back as the whiffle ball ricochets off of his designer desk.

"So now why are you here?" he asks as he slams another one into a nearby wall.

"I'd like to bring my clients over and be an agent here," I say directly.

"You're just not what we're about," he says, bending his knees just so. "I am really trying to work on my alignment," he continues. I sit for a moment and watch a couple of practice swings to be polite, and then get up. "See ya," he says as I walk out of his office.

Cross off that agency. I walk along Wilshire Boulevard in the blinding California light trying to ready myself for the next meeting. It is all about mental preparation, or not.

The founding partner here is an old beau. "Well, they all come back eventually," he snarls as I trudge in the door trying to sweat discreetly. "So you got any clients I've ever heard of?" he asks as I read the names off my list.

"Surely you recognize the names of the ones I stole from you," I retort.

"Same old Maria," he comments as he ushers me out the door. If only I had dated more carefully.

So on to the next. "You just really don't add any value here.

We have an older woman agent," the kid who owns this agency tells me.

"Right," I say as I make my way to the door.

And then I am sitting in the agency of all agencies feeling even smaller than I am. Equally diminished by the architecture and the day. This one has got to work out. I am nervous. The man I am seeing is the One That Got Away. The man I stopped seeing because I wanted him too much. I try to fluff up and smooth out my little black dress that is getting tighter by the moment. I wish I had never dated agents to begin with, but who knew?

He looks great and has an appealing spring in his step. And he has actually gotten up and come out of his office to greet me. Where is it that you go for that Do-Over?

"So, you're getting married," I say.

"Yeah." He beams. "What brings you out here?"

"Well, actually, I need a job," I say.

"Not here?" he asks/tells me.

And then I am back out on Wilshire, fresh out of talent agencies, feeling as if I might puke. Could this be the day I got fired from show business? I head for the airport in need of my three thousand miles and another plan.

APRIL 24

"I am not supposed to attend," I tell Jed as I walk back into my office forty-eight hours since my last exit.

"No takers?" he asks.

"Nada," I reply, trying to sound upbeat and unconcerned. "Oh yeah, and I am pregnant."

My little assistant runs into my office and closes the door behind him. "Are we going to have another conversation about boundaries?" he asks.

"I told you, I failed boundaries," I exclaim.

"Oh, God, Maria," he says, concerned.

"Yeah, well, it will all work out," I say, trying to rearrange the furniture of my brain one more time.

APRIL 26 I am seated in the oh-so-private inner sanctum of Bergdorf's very own personal shopper. "What do you think of this one?" Wyatt asks as she trots out of the dressing room in yet another little black dress.

I sip my mint tea thoughtfully. "It's chic, but not of much import," I say, carefully considering my words. So this is shopping with the rich and famous. Betty, the personal shopper, has amassed every little black dress in the store, arranged them in order of potential preference, and hung them in a special secret dressing room. They were waiting when we arrived.

"I really appreciate you doing this, Maria. I don't know what's wrong with me, I can't seem to make my mind up about anything these days," Wyatt confesses.

"I am happy to be here," I say as I stuff a chocolate truffle into my mouth.

Wyatt struts out in a T-shirty number with cleavage. "A little L.A." I smile.

"Well, it's black anyway." Wyatt smiles.

"You know, Maria, I really need to do something creative," Wyatt explains through the dressing room door.

"Creative?" I ask. She is now modeling a very conservative coatdress. "A little too Jackie O," I tell her.

"I need to write a book or make a movie, or possibly a documentary—you know, so I'll have something that's mine to talk about at all of these black-tie dinners," she continues. "But it's not like I have the time to do such a thing; maybe we could do something together."

Sure, lady, I could dash off a Broadway hit, maybe a musical with political underpinnings that ought to add a little dimension to your dinner party repartee. "I see," I say, hoping she'll forget this notion and move on to another topic.

"How's it going with Harry?" she asks as she parades out of the dressing room in the perfect hint of a black dress.

"You look beautiful," I say, truly meaning it.

"Thanks," she says. "I guess this one is a keeper."

I think about telling her I am pregnant, but think better of it. "Harris is okay," I say.

"Well, you know, Maria, a woman is so much better with a man. Get this one to marry you," she instructs. Will do. That is, right after I dash off that Tony Award winner with both of our names on the title page. "Oh, my God, I have got to run," she says while gathering up a couple of selections and heading for the elevator. "I loved seeing you," she says as the elevator doors are closing. "Don't forget. Get Harry to marry you," she reiterates, and then she is gone. And I am alone in Bergdorf's thinking about walking back to the office.

APRIL 27 I am standing in the fish market in Wainscott with a preening Harris feeling fat and tired, so tired. We are back in the Hamptons being domestic. "Definitely the sea bass," Harris says with the most commitment that I have seen him muster in months. Thank God he believes in something.

He's mad at me because I vetoed weekend guests so now we're stuck with each other for two days and it's harder to deny my existence when he keeps running into me. The fish smell is making me more nauseous than usual. But since I don't exist it should be impossible for me to throw up. At least that's what I keep telling myself out by the road bent over retching into the cool sea-doused air.

And then we drive over to Shelter Island. We're running in a nature conservancy and I can't keep up, and I watch as Harris runs away from me. Up a little hill and then he is lost in the trees. I feel the earth beneath me sinking fast because I know I can't catch him and I fear I've run out of tricks.

"The fish is good," he says.

"Yeah," I say as he digs into the salad greens, and there is just the two of us and the sound of crunching. And I just can't seem to ask. What about this baby, and you and me and love and life? I think it really hard, but the telepathy line must be down because he just keeps crunching. And I keep thinking and the doorbell rings, and he gets up and answers the door. And presto, two of the whitest people I have ever seen.

"Tad and Alix, this is Maria," Harris announces.

"Hello," I say with a smile, employing my best agent tones.

"Hey," they say in unison.

"They're in my running club in the city," Harris explains. Oh, joy.

"Great," I say. "Will you have some dessert?"

And so I serve crumble to the two most boring white people in the Western Hemisphere. "That's marathon running," she keeps saying as The Mister describes in excruciating detail about his hamstring tear and knee weakness, and the hills and valleys, and fits and starts of seeing the world while running a five-minute mile. Harris is rapt, and I think maybe they are speaking code and if I could just get the handbook it would all become clear.

And then when there is no more crumble they disappear, and Harris says the most extraordinary thing in a wistful tone: "Didn't you always think you'd wind up marrying someone like them?"

"No," I say. He doesn't respond.

He retires to bed to read *Runner's World*. I am having none of this. I crawl into the king-size country bed and slowly and carefully remove the magazine from his hands, and replace that diversion with one of my own making. He doesn't complain. And then when we are both completely exhausted our entwined bodies drift off to a state of unconsciousness.

APRIL 28 I am lying in bed alone. Sunday morning, the house is quiet. Harris is probably out for a run. I am debating whether or not to get up. It is warm and safe here, but my curiosity wins out. I pull on a pair of sweats, a T-shirt, and my afterski boots and head out of the bedroom. "Harris," I call. No answer. No activity in the kitchen. I head to the front door.

I stand on the front porch, and there in full view is Harris. He is standing on the gravel driveway. His back is to me. He is wearing khaki shorts, a T-shirt, and his running shoes without socks. I feel a proprietary surge of affection as my eyes take in the taut little balls, one on each leg, that are his calf muscles.

He is pissing into the rosebushes that line the driveway. I remain quiet. He shakes off, zips up, and turns toward the house. "Why do men do that?" I ask, referring to his insistent peeing out of doors.

"Because we can." He smiles.

"Want to go for a run?" I ask.

"I am taking a day off from running today. It is part of my training," he says in sacrosanct tones.

"Want to go out for breakfast?" I try again.

"Not really," he says.

That one hurt. "Well, I will make you Sunday breakfast here then. French toast."

"I only like French toast one particular way, and we don't have the right bread here," he says.

I refuse to give in to this. "Well, maybe you'll find out you like it two ways," I say hopefully.

"Not worth the risk," he jets back.

"Harris, there is hardly great risk involved here," I say, standing my ground.

He walks past me into the house. Now I am feeling a little desperate. The man would rather marry the couple from his running club than me, and he is sure I can't pull off French toast.

"Ah, come on," I say as I slide my arms around his waist and plant my head on his chest. "Just try my French toast," I say into his warm, flat, stomach.

"Okay," he says. "I'll take a shower, you make the French toast."

I whisk the eggs and milk into a frenzy in the chipped red bowl that we usually reserve for tuna fish salad. I take it as a good omen when I find an old iron griddle in one of the drawers that holds pots and pans. "This one came with the house," I say aloud.

"What?" shouts Harris from the bathroom.

"Nothing. Just talking to myself," I yell back.

"Don't do that," he yells back joylessly.

I douse two generously sliced pieces of thick French bread into the gooey mixture. "This is going to be good," I sing out before I remember the statute against unilateral conversations. I am safe. He did not hear me. I hear the shower running. I add a little more vanilla to the goo and douse the bread again. The butter on the griddle sizzles. The smell of French toast wafts through the house and melds with the smell of cold fresh air. I smile in contemplation of my victory.

"I can't eat this. The bread is too fat," Harris says as he winces with rage.

"The maple syrup is really good. It's from Vermont. I got it at a vegetable stand on Route 27," I practically sing to drown out his displeasure. Harris looks down at his plate with disgust and says nothing. He is not eating.

"I don't think it is supposed to be this hard," I finally say when I can stand the silence no longer.

"I know," he says as he pats my left arm. "I know."

MAY 2 I am sitting in the office looking out at rooftops and the buildings below. International-style facades smashed up against nineteenth-century fantasies and dusk. I am in love with someone I don't know yet. I am filled with fear and optimism—and fatigue—about this baby. Jed calls out, "Harris on line one."

"Hi," I say.

"I got invited up to Maine," he says proudly. Mr. Social Register comes through.

"Great, Harris," I say.

"So you'll come, right?" he asks.

"Of course," I say, really touched by my inclusion.

"And Maria . . ."

"Yes?" I say, thinking about what clothes I have that I can still wear.

"Let's just pretend you're not pregnant, so we can just relax and enjoy the weekend, okay?"

"Sure," I say, stunned.

And then Jed calls out, "The Grand Poo Bah on line two."

"Hey, Harris, my boss is on the other line," I say.

"Love you," he says. And he is gone. It is the first time Harris has ever uttered the word *love* and so I think I feel better about everything as I pick up line two.

"Maria, I am coming into New York and would like to schedule a time to meet with you," The Grand Poo Bah commands. And there it is, the end of my career as I know it.

"Yes, of course," I say. And then I go back to staring out the window at the waning day, and trying to convince myself that it's not what I think.

MAY 6 Although it is not expressly stated both Harris and I know what he really wants is a tall blonde model who heels and does not bark, and who is a superior athlete. I live with La Fantaisie. And Harris lives without her. And that is the deal. Until recently I thought that this was a most unsatisfactory arrangement and then I began to think that perhaps the reason I put up with Harris is not so much because I love him or even because I am carrying his child, but because I am competitive. I aim to beat out Fantasy Girl. I will outcook her, outdress her, and certainly give a better blow job than she would ever hope to or perhaps consent to give. With my superior intelligence and agent's ability to put up with shit I will just plain outlast her. I may not be taller and blonder, but I am tougher and wiser and more determined than a pack of fantasy girls, and for this reason I will win.

At least I hope I will as I gently caress Harris out of sleep and into arousal. The Monday morning blow job, a tender reminder that not all Monday morning activities are loathsome. I wait for him to shiver and groan, and then it is time to start the day. He runs off to jog in the park, and I run to work, for that most loathsome of Monday's activities, the Monday morning staff meeting.

"You're late," The Radical Theatre Agent announces as he stares me down in the hall.

Well, you know, with the blow job, finding just the right outfit, blowing out my hair, putting on a little war paint, eating some cereal, taking a last look at the seven scripts I carted home and failed to read, and then waiting for the B train there just doesn't seem to be enough time. "Sorry," I say, not even bothering with the explanation. If you can't read my mind you just don't get to know.

I find my place at the long table with the rest of the Gang Who Can't Shoot Straight, look across the table, and there seated across from me is Eddie Munster. I never noticed before, but one of the newer talent agents is a dead ringer for Eddie. I smile and he smiles back. The resemblance is uncanny. I try not laughing, but the more I try the more convulsed I am. And then we are experiencing technical difficulties with London, and so Tuesday will become Monday, and the entire day is canceled, at least teleconferencing-wise. It all should work out sometime tomorrow, late afternoon. That is, if the West Coast gets hooked up and beamed across a continent or so. We all file out. Saved by the bell. Baby Harris and I are laughing our asses off because the Gang Who Can't Shoot Straight includes Eddie Munster.

"Too much laughing," The Radical Theatre Agent comments as he glides past me in the hall on the long walk back to our little offices to start the week. I step into my office without responding. The Radical Theatre Agent is superfluous, as are the rest of these Bozos. There is a person inside of me and I have got to find another job.

I head down in the elevator, and out into the pedestrian stream. My head is filled with worry and lack of possibility. Why am I unable to make my life work? How can I transform myself into a woman that both the agency and Harris desire? "I must keep going," I say aloud into the sea of bodies before me. The rest of it just doesn't matter. Or at least that is my take as I rush through the crowded streets to meet my luncheon companion at her club in the East Fifties. Will I ever be able to hail a fucking cab?

Now I am late and there is nothing I can do but keep running. As I ride up in the elevator in some nondescript high-rise I wonder just what kind of a club this is, and who it is that belongs here? A bland dining room is all I encounter, and then, a sixty-something woman who is not used to being kept waiting. I will disarm her with my charm. Or not. I sit down with a thud. Her expression suggests that this will not be easy.

Judith Sweetzer was once a nun, then the head of a cable network. She presently runs a charitable foundation. She has one of those New York husbands who was once the head of something. She has agreed to meet me, but insisted it be at her club. We have met in passing at sit-down dinners, at proper parties in the Hamptons, and at fashion do's. She has a kind face. She is always manicured and elegant. And there is the nun thing. Surely she will help me.

"I am thinking of leaving the agency and am interested in utilizing my skills in another area, perhaps a charitable foundation," I begin with hopeful precision.

"Are you quite wealthy, my dear?" she responds.

"No," I say, not sure where we are going here.

"What man are you with?" she asks, continuing her interrogation.

"I am seeing a—"

"You're not married?" she says with disapproval.

Okay, lady, so I am not a closer. "No," I respond.

"You're not married. You have no real money, and you are contemplating leaving your job?" she asks.

"Well, I—" I try again.

"Wake up," the ex-nun intones. "You need to marry the most powerful man you can find. You need a job that will allow you to amass a significant amount of capital. Then we will talk charities," she says. She is finished. And so it appears am I. She looks at her watch before brusquely getting up from the table.

I am simultaneously cold and perspiring as I make my way along West Fifty-seventh Street en route to the office. The words *amass capital* scream in my head. I think about dashing into one of the elegant office buildings along the way. I will smash the glass of the fire alarm. I will grab a megaphone from a passing firefighter. They do carry those, don't they? "Okay, only the most powerful men need line up," I'll command. "Are any of you guys available?" I'll ask. The first one that nods yes and is semi-appealing wins. I'll just grab him, and take my rightful place among those that give freely to charity. *No problema.*

When I enter my office Jed jumps up from his post. "You need to call the Malibu Sheriff's station immediately," he says. He is white. All of the blood has drained from his face.

"My family?" I ask.

"No—Barry Hovington," he says.

"Dead?" I say.

"I don't think so," he says. And then I am dialing.

"Are you Barry Hovington's agent?" the appropriate official demands.

"Yes. I am," I say, still unclear as to Barry's whereabouts.

"After a high-speed chase he is in a standoff with the police out here in Malibu. He has broken into a private home. Do you think he could be armed?" he asks.

"Doubtful," I say, still trying to process the information.

"He wants to talk to you," he continues. "We are going to radio you in."

"Okay," I say.

"Go ahead," the official implores.

"Barry," I begin.

"Darling," he slurs. "Do you think I should remove all of my clothes?" He is not that wasted. He is thinking of premovie publicity for his pitch.

"No, B. Give yourself up and I'll get you an attorney. Don't say anything more to anybody," I instruct.

"You sound so serious, old girl," he further slurs in a chatty sort of way.

"Barry!" I scream to get his attention.

"Right," he says more seriously now. "I am giving up," I hear Barry say. And then I am cut off. I hope they don't kill him.

I call a well-known criminal defense attorney. I call the agency's legal department and the internal public relations department. Then I call the publicist to the stars and spin a tale. "This is gonna cost ya, babe," she laughs while taking it all down.

"Whatever," I snap. Then I call all of the columnists and talk show hosts I know personally. Jed calls the assistants of the ones we don't know to alert them that something big is going down and that they should have their bosses call me.

"Barry Hovington is the brilliant South African writer-director who just sold the Naked Man pitch for a couple of million," I begin. "He's a method writer," I continue in a jovial tone all the while praying he locked himself up in that house long enough for his blood alcohol level to go down. I wonder how much more of this Baby Harris and I can stand.

There are no boundaries in this line of work. We are all the functionally insane. And that is on a good day. I think we should all be forced to change jobs every few years. I'll be the filmmaker and Barry can be the savior/agent and The Radical Theatre Agent can finally do musical comedy.

It is late now. Barry is in the clink with a superlative international legal team behind him and a potential booking on Letterman. That is, if we can manage to get him out of jail before the public forgets who he is.

I hug Jed out on the street. "Thanks, buddy," I say, about to burst into tears.

"Long day," he sighs as he heads down into the subway. He is very late for a date down in SoHo.

"She's still waiting," I add as he disappears from sight.

I head up to Fairway on foot. I don't even care that there are no cabs. The air feels good. I am meeting Harris, who also worked late tonight. I find him in the produce department.

"Hey," I say.

"Hey," he says and smiles.

I want to tell him about Eddie Munster, and the ex-nun, and the police standoff, and somehow it comes out, "I love you, Harris." Right there in front of the navel oranges and everyone. And then I force myself to look directly into his eyes. And I see only disappointment. And I think of our little baby, and I vow to try harder at making eggs, runny not stiff. At better vacuuming, at long-distance running, at being more loving, more supportive, more organized, less loquacious, taller, blonder.

"Do you want beets?" he responds.

We decide to take all of the food down to Harris's place. As we struggle out the door of the market, laden with bags, a cab pulls right up to the curb in front of us. Harris jumps into the cab without giving its almost magical appearance a moment's notice. Why is that?

I am stirring polenta in a copper pot on Harris's fancy burners. We have decided on soft cornmeal with three cheeses, baby food for our late-night dinner. Harris has put on a CD. Soft music wafts through the loft. He comes up behind me and gently wraps his arms around my waist. He smells fresh. He pulls me closer, and I feel myself melt into him. I feel his warmth. I feel connected. I am sure he must feel this too. At least I hope he does. We finish the meal. I have not referred to any of the specifics of my day. I am too tired for that.

I am the last one to pile into bed. The coolness of the soft cotton sheets feels cleansing. I am drifting off when Harris pulls me toward him. His kisses are soft and kind. He gently brushes my hair behind my ears.

"You are my love," he whispers. I think that is what he said. He wraps himself around me. My body forms a line down the middle of his torso and we become one. I feel thoughts of how much I love him fill every part of him and me, and briefly we are safe from everything.

MAY 7 Barry is sitting in jail and I have gotten a reprieve, or so the message reads. The Grand Poo Bah has postponed our meeting. "Maria, heard you on CNN last night. Tough situation. Won't be coming to New York next week. We'll have to reschedule." *Click*.

The Radical Theatre Agent saunters over to my door. "The Grand Poo Bah, eh?" he comments.

"Yeah," I say.

"So, Maria, would you like to join me at the theater tonight? It's a preview," he inquires/invites.

"Gee, I'd love to, but I guess I have to see how the day plays out. He's still in custody," I say, milking this one for all its worth.

"Yes, of course," The Radical Theatre Agent responds, all grown-up business now. He marches off. And for my next trick.

"Let's order the lattes," I cry out to Jed.

"Maria, you're pushing it," he yells back in between answering lines. Jed looks exhausted. It is barely 9 A.M. in L.A. All four lines are flashing. "Barry on line two," he yells.

"I am still in fucking lockup," Barry informs me.

"Yeah, well, the high-speed chase thing always complicates matters," I snap back. Never give the recalcitrant client an edge.

"Christ," snaps Barry.

Now for the more maternal tone. "We are going to get you out, B. Hang tough," I say.

"Maria, it wasn't really a break-in," he says.

"Yeah?" I say.

"It was my former agent's beach house," Barry admits with a hint of embarrassment.

"You ran to the last fucking Bozo?" I demand, a little hurt.

"Well, you don't have a fucking Malibu beach house last time I looked," whines Barry.

"Touché," I say. "I am sure he won't press charges."

"Well, he's pretty mad at me," Barry whines.

"Got it," I say. "I'll see what I can do."

"And get me the fuck out of here," Barry instructs.

"Okay," I say.

"Got to go," he says.

"Yeah," I say.

"Well, well, well," clucks the fat Armani suit on the other end of the line.

"Hey, Marty," I say.

"Client problems?" He laughs.

"You're not going to press charges are you, buddy?" I ask.

"We have to share the commission on all of this Naked business, take it or leave it," he snaps back.

"You have got to be kidding," I scream.

"Couldn't be more serious," he answers.

"Jed, get me a meeting with Business Affairs pronto!" I scream.

"Namaste," Mr. Business Affairs' assistant, Jamalle, greets me. We haven't really encountered each other since my night with the shaman.

"Yeah," I say, not really interested in being teased at the moment.

I am ushered in. Mr. Business Affairs (Julius, to his friends) looks out at me over his half glasses, over his stacks of files, and over a desk so large it looks as if it might take off.

"We have to cut Barry Hovington's last agency in on the Naked deal," I launch in.

"Really?" Mr. Business Affairs questions. The subtext is clear. No fucking way.

"Barry has been arrested," I try to continue, but he cuts me off.

"Yes, I caught you talking him down last night on CNN," he barks. "Very impressive. It's always something with you, isn't it, Maria?" he sneers.

Now I am mad. Mad with no leverage. A pervasive condition these days. I begin to count to ten in French. *"Un, deux, trois,"* I utter in whispered tones.

"Excuse me?" says Mr. Business Affairs, taking control, snapping me back into his ken.

"They want a fifty-fifty split, but I think I can get them down," I interject optimistically.

"Or what?" Mr. Business Affairs asks.

"Or the managing partner presses charges for breaking and entering, exacerbating our client's situation," I state, trying for diplomacy. What would Amy Vanderbilt have to say about this one?

"You mean or you're A-list client hangs his sorry ass in jail?" he asks, attempting to gain clarity.

"Something like that," I mumble.

"Let him rot," Mr. Business Affairs barks. "I've heard it is very conducive to writing," he says, looking back down at the papers on his desk.

"Ah, come on, Julius," I implore. This is going to be a very long day.

"Let's just bring in our sleeping bags," Jed suggests as we settle in for another late night. The Judge will set bail for Barry's release, but only if he goes straight to Rehab. Barry is adamant that he wants Rehab in the Malibu Colony. I am calling in every favor since the fifth grade to pull this one out of my hat.

"Heavy breathing on line three," Jed calls out. The kid is slaphappy.

"Hello," I say into the receiver, hoping to speak to my mother's friend Marge, whose nephew is a wealthy alumnus of Malibu Colony Rehab.

"I've got my cock in my hand," groans the unidentified caller.

Jeez. "Bingham got fired, pal, and we're not interested," I firmly state into the phone before slamming down the receiver.

"Thanks, Jed," I call out.

"Full service," he laughs.

"Damn straight," I howl. I should have asked the heavy breather if he wants to come back to our agency. Next time. "Jed, get Marty What's-His-Name on the line," I shriek with delight.

"Hey, Buddy," I say.

"What'll it be, Maria?" he snaps back.

"Hard day?" I ask.

"Whatever," he says.

"Are you folks ready to pony up?" he arrogantly snarls.

"Not exactly, Marty. You see, one of your biggest clients—you know, the one who likes to make dirty phone calls—just phoned in, and I may have accidentally recorded it," I say as politely as possible under the circumstances.

"Oh, fuck," old Marty sighs. "Let's just call it a draw."

"Beautiful," I say. "Nice doing business with you."

MAY 9 I am in a cab careening down Seventh Avenue. The driver smells of garlic, perspiration, and an herb I cannot identify. Cumin? It could be cumin or maybe saffron. Baby Harris does not like to be jostled.

"Excuse me," I call out at the driver, who seems to be weaving through traffic just for the hell of it. No answer.

"Excuse me," I try again a little more frantically. Still no answer.

"Hey, Buddy, I may puke all over the back seat," I bellow. The driver screeches to a halt. Oh, this is whiplash.

"Get out of my cab!" screams the driver. "Get out now," he commands. "No puking in my cab. No puking." He clearly has rules. I wonder what accent that is as I climb out of the tin box that has whipped me around like a washing machine.

I am meant to meet Harris on a corner in SoHo. We are en route to a fundraiser for an art institute. I didn't ask how he scored these tickets, but I am quite sure it will be filled with society types with whom Harris longs to be associated. I am in no mood. But I haven't seen Harris in two days on account of all of the Barry drama, and it feels awful. I am longing for him. Baby Harris and I need to see him. It feels rigged. I am carrying his genetic material, and so now I have longing. What next?

"Jesus God, you're late," barks Harris as I climb out of a cab onto West Broadway. "Well, I got stuck in that no-man's-land between midtown and the Village and I couldn't find a cab," I begin.

"The subway," he mutters. "The subway."

I say nothing. We start walking in tandem. There are no words. Harris ploughs on ahead. I am trying hard to keep up, but I am losing. Finally I just stop. After a few more paces Harris turns.

"What?" he demands.

"What yourself?" I say back.

He waits and makes a little hand signal ushering me toward him. My high heels are too tight. I focus on the radiating pain coming from the corn on my right pinky, and I do what I am told.

"You know, Maria, you could have told me about Hovington," he says.

"What?" I say. Harris is fighting back rage. I am in the midst of another car crash. What is going on here?

"I am in the Reality Business," he barks. "How do you think I feel when I have to learn you were on fucking CNN from some intern at work?"

My own rage takes an express elevator. "Gee, Harris, I couldn't remember if we were just ignoring the pregnancy or my job too? It gets confusing," I snap back. You want to play tennis? We'll play tennis.

There is thirty seconds of staring and breathing. And then a sound. A piercing birdcall of a sound and I am shaking with sobs. I cry for the imprisoned Barry, the exhausted Jed, the furious Harris, and for helpless little Baby Harris.

"Shit," I say, wishing we could just sneak away to Raoul's for *dîner à deux* and knowing that yet another performance is required.

It is a New York party, all right. A few recognizable notables from the world of arts and letters, models, super and aging, a couple of minor Kennedys, an independent film star (if there is such a thing), a celebrity chef, and plenty of money, i.e., starving-looking women accompanied by bored well-turned-out men, and us pressing our noses against the Plexiglas. Harris makes a beeline toward someone I vaguely recognize, a fashion designer, I think, and of course away from me. I head for the bar, and a nonalcoholic drink—Baby Harris doesn't appreciate booze, not yet anyway.

From my perch I survey the room to see if there is anyone I should be signing. Why waste a perfectly good party? And I am caught, defenseless, peering out over the sea of heads. I have forgotten to watch my back.

"Hey, there." Fin, The Evil Leprechaun, smiles.

"Hi," I say, trying to look as if I have seen someone in the crowd and it is of the utmost importance.

He's not buying it. "So you made the news," he comments.

"Not really. It's all about the clients," I say, wanting to get away. Shouldn't he be stargazing or something? Why me?

"And their agents," he chirps.

I do not merit this obsequious tone. Take a powder, pal. "Not really," I firmly state.

"So you and Harris have been seein' each other a while," he continues. I smell danger. Harris thinks this guy is his friend. There is no jealousy like an Irishman. "Ya know, the other day Harris asked me if ya should let someone tell you that they love ya when you yourself are not sure," he says like a viper. "And I told him absolutely you should."

I am hit. He has fired a cannonball at close range. I feel the heavy lead ball thrust into me. There is that brief unfeeling moment. And then pain in all directions.

Just then Harris walks up, pleased as punch, with a preeminent male ballet dancer in tow. I remember he is Spanish. *"Buenas noches,"* I say with all of my *th*es in place. I lightly pat his dangling right arm. I want to tell him I know he is a trapped party favor. I think it very hard and smile gently in his direction.

Perhaps the telepathy lines are working. His eyes dart, looking for an exit. Both Harris and Fin stand too close to him and look up at him adoringly. Their hungry expressions are almost sexual. I slam that door immediately. I cannot afford any thoughts in that direction, not one.

"We're all going dancing up in Harlem after this," Harris announces, The Little Cruise Director.

I look at the dancer and he looks at me. Over his dead something. The telepathy lines are definitely running.

"I'll have to opt out," I say. "I am just too tired."

Harris glowers in my direction: You ruin everything. The telepathy lines again.

"Me too," says the ballet dancer, jumping away in a start. He has escaped back into the social swirl, an unrecognizable spec in its midst.

"Well, Fin and I and the others in our group are going," Harris informs me. What group is that?

"Okay," I say. "I think I'll just head on uptown."

"Okay," he says.

"We can drop her on our way," says Fin. The evil kid in the class who never gets caught. I wait in my viselike shoes for "the group" to decide it is time to go.

It is late at night. I am lounging in the window seat of my apartment, floating eleven floors above the mayhem. I stare across at the planetarium. I love it here. I am clutching at a mountain of sand. I must make a plan.

MAY 20 "Hi, I am in a car to the airport," I say.

"How long are you gone for?" Harris asks. I search for some emotion in his voice.

"Got to check on Barry, a couple of meetings," I semi-explain.

"How long?" he asks again. Insistence, no love.

"Couple of days," I respond.

Cell phone static, no love. "Harris?" I say, demonstrating an edge of desperation. Damn.

"Yeah?" he says. More cell phone static, still no love.

"Maria, let's just be kind to each other," he finally says.

"Yeah, okay," I say.

More static. A standoff.

"Bye," I say.

"Yeah, bye," he says. But what about love?

MAY 21 I have scheduled a meeting with a talent agency located in the same building as a Mercedes dealership. It is not on Wilshire. It is not several floors, but it has cachet. Translation, it has a lot of big moneymaking television clients. Show Runners—not horses that run around a track, but head writers on sitcoms and nighttime serial dramas that rake in millions of dollars annually, *ka-ching*.

I am sitting in the little waiting area. Air and space and light. Assistants with desks almost big enough to take off. The smell of money. "Would you like some Evian? Perrier?" The pretty assistant speaks in California slur. Slow loping words; no point really, just casually amassing millions. Baby Harris and I might like it here.

I meet their senior partner, Le Grand Fromage, in their conference room. Smaller than ours, but sufficient. "I will call in the group after our conversation," Le Grand Fromage informs me. I think I remember this one used to be a public defender.

Long way to the Criminal Courts Building, eh, buddy? Could this be the same "group" Harris took dancing up in Harlem? Doubtful. A West Coast chapter? Perhaps. Men and their groups. Are there directories? If so I need to see one immediately. Wall-to-wall Armani, and then—The Conversation.

Fits and starts. It is not going well. He says a name. I am meant to identify the person and their show. I get some, but not all. I was supposed to have memorized their client list. Who knew?

"I am really a movie person," I weakly explain.

This guy wears his success all the way to his teeth. There is no excuse for not knowing the names that made him rich. Perhaps you speak Hugo Boss and I have been speaking Armani. Did I tell you I am bilingual? *Hugo Boss,* I meditate. Only a busy signal.

And now for the group. They file in. The mean boys in the Armani suits and their one token woman, an aging character dressed in a kimono and combat boots. They all just stare.

"You're not really an agent, are you?" demands Le Grand Fromage.

MAY 22 I am speeding along Pacific Coast Highway en route to Malibu. More air, and light, not hot, not cold, just perfection. I am meant to see Barry in rehab, well, actually we're meeting in a swank restaurant located in a parking lot, a California phenomenon. I swing the agency's loaner Mercedes into the sparkling lot. Everyone is wearing shorts and expensive sunglasses. No particular hurry, no rushing to judgment, or anywhere.

I settle into a booth, attempting to look prosperous. The restaurant is Malibu kitsch, bad vinyl décor, hefty prices, and microscopic portions. Barry teeters in very slowly with handlers, one on each side. After depositing Barry they position themselves strategically near our booth.

"They are guarding our lunch," Barry explains.

"I can't drink either," I commence, trying for solidarity.

"What's your excuse?" the wavering Barry inquires.

"Pregnant," I say.

"Good work, old girl. Do we know the father?"

"Vaguely," I respond.

Now it is I who wants to touch Barry. He looks smaller without his poisons, so much more vulnerable.

"Any packaging possibilities in Malibu Colony Prep?" I inquire as Barry attempts to get the water glass to his lips.

Just a shrug. "Haven't met the housemates yet," he explains. Tears brim at his eyes' edges. I try a reassuring smile. "This is a fine fucking mess," he says as though he has just this moment assessed the situation.

"Not so bad," I say.

"The chase was brilliant," Barry says faintly. "Fucking brilliant."

MAY 23 I meander about the agency's cavernous Los Angeles office. No! The audience yells. Not toward the danger! It is a horror film. The Grand Poo Bah's number two assistant ushers me into the office. And there he is. Flossed and brushed and shined. In control. Manning his craft. I take a seat. Ready to copilot. Praying I still have a mission.

"Maria, good to have you out here," he says. "How's Barry?"

"Doing well," I say with confidence. Flashing on frail Barry being led away by burly handlers. "Doing well," I say it again to erase the image.

"Good," he says. "It's all propitious." The Grand Poo Bah loves words. He is not always certain where to put them. I smile and nod. Baby Harris and I need a job.

"We're having a small retreat," he continues. "I'd like you to join us. It's an invective," he adds. Now he's lost me. What could he mean by invective?

"Great," I say. Brevity is definitely the bet here.

MAY 25 We are hunkered down in the basement of a seaside hotel being positive. Airless, windowless, and upbeat.

"You need to believe to achieve," we state in unison. And then people witness. A Quaker meeting, Hollywood style.

"I really loved Schwarzenegger's work. I believed. And I signed him," someone offers. The crowd goes wild.

"I believe I will sign Brad Pitt," someone else offers.

"You have to believe to achieve," we all say back.

"I signed Woody Allen," someone else shouts out.

"Did you believe?" the Grand Poo Bah demands.

"Yes, I did," says the agent.

"And you achieved," the Grand Poo Bah answers.

I am concentrating on not being cynical. Baby Harris needs me to believe and achieve or we may starve. I can't help but wonder if the next event of the day might not be a fire walk. Excuse me, are pregnant women allowed to walk over burning coals? I myself have misplaced the literature on that one, and besides I have a plane to catch.

MAY 26 Where does one sign up to go AWOL from one's own life? Baby Harris and I are fresh out of plans. The lush New York spring is everywhere. The town car makes its way down Fifth Avenue and then across the park and home. The thought of complete reinvention is exhausting. I love Harris. It's the group I am not so sure about. The weekend with Mr. Social Register looms large. Still no discussion of my agency contract being renewed. I need to sign a movie star and get my name in the social register to comfortably inhabit my own life. Not impossible. I am believing, but the jury seems to be out on the achieving. No flashes of loneliness. Just concern for my own group, Baby Harris and me. As I unlock the door to my apartment I hear my phone's incessant ring, my outgoing message, and then a dial tone. Let him wonder. I hope it is not too late for dating games. My strategy is waning.

I am too tortured to sleep. I pull on my running clothes and head out for an early morning run in the park. My thoughts are grinding. I am coming to the end of a mound of fluff. I have chased stars for a living and boyfriends for sport. I fear show business may be divorcing me. I have a metallic taste in my mouth. A general aching that is the guaranteed result of the red-eye. The moisture in the air wipes away a layer of fatigue. The relentless pounding of my feet against the pavement soothes the fear. I have no Plan B. The chase is on.

Harris must believe he is chasing me as I surreptitiously corner him. And then there he is coming toward me. Running clockwise. Fighting the general counterclockwise flow. Gliding past the old tanned jogger, two pudgy psychotherapists, and a lean thoroughbred of a woman. My heart pounds. I try to mold my dry lips in the direction of a smile. I completely inhabit my yearning. And then he is past. Did he not see me? I move to the periphery of the dirt path and turn. Did he not see me? I focus on his coarse black hair and muscular legs. I watch his rapid movements. He becomes smaller. A thing in the distance. And then he is gone, and I am bereft. Did he not see me?

Perhaps I am unseen because I exist on a parallel plane. I stop at Dr. Drink's office to learn that Baby Harris has been promoted to a new trimester. Harris has erased me, and Baby Harris is eating me from the inside out. Perhaps it is because I am not successful enough that I have disappeared. I walk down Park Avenue toward the office noticing only achievers. Maybe the unsuccessful do exist here, they are just invisible. New

York is a city of achievement and if you fail to achieve—poof, you vanish. What is it I am meant to achieve? Invisibility brings clarity. The clients are purses that talk. Merchandise to be moved. And I am the seller. If I am unable to sell enough I run out of ink. First I was something, now nothing.

But how does one fight it, this invisibility thing? I look around at all those who clearly exist, sharply dressed Upper East Side women, businessmen, the occasional idiosyncratic character. Shop, amass money, create a Broadway show? I am, therefore I spend, I amass, I create? I feel more tired than I have ever felt. The Red-Eye, the Baby, the Job, oh, God. I summon all of my residual strength. I march into the office intent upon thwarting my own disappearance.

"Barry on line two," Jed announces in a somber tone.

"I am dying in here," Barry begins.

"Any pretty young inmates to play J. C. Izod's adulterous lover?" I inquire.

"Oh, please," gasps Barry.

"Just trying to leverage the situation," I try to explain.

"I can't stand it here," screams Barry.

"Okay, okay, what's wrong with it?" An agent should always make things better.

"Well, it's so fucking sunny," Barry yells. For a brooding alcoholic that probably would be a problem.

"I see," I say. "Can you just sit there and write?"

Then a pause that is too long.

"Barry?" I say.

"You just don't get it," he says. Then another long pause.

"I do," I say, filled with my own fear and uncertainty. "I'll think of something," I offer.

"You better," he says. Then a *click.* I stare at the inactive phone, waiting for inspiration.

I walk over to Radu, a private gym on West Fifty-seventh Street, and jump on the treadmill. I am believing so where is the achieving? A supermodel, a fashion designer, and a TV star are my gym mates. Bored eastern European trainers count out beats to individualized torture. Vun, tew, tree, vun, tew, tree, vun, tew . . . I should send Harris and his TV crew to film Barry in Malibu Rehab. Now there would be some reality programming. If Barry took a piece of the show (I mean, it is his rehab after all) and if it were to go into syndication Barry would never have to worry about money again. Barry's annuity funded by his rehab—not bad, I think as I move on to sit-ups.

The idea of a despondent Barry lighting up for the camera makes me smile.

Episode 1 The House Tour
Episode 2 The Housemates
Episode 3 Barry's First AA Meeting
Episode 4 Barry Takes Responsibility for His Actions
Episode 5 Barry Is Sentenced by the Judge
Episode 6 Barry and the "Houseguests" Put On a Show for Charity

Reality programming, meet reality. It's got to be better than watching some debutante eat live beetles in Polynesia. The more sit-ups I do the more this is sounding like a very good idea. Who says a pregnant woman can't exercise?

Episode 7 Barry and the Other Houseguests Go into Malibu to Do Some Shopping. . . .

JUNE 12 And then I am back in the unflattering light. One can make their dreams come true, at least in prime time. I am standing in the garden of the Bel Air Hotel watching the swans. I am waiting for Harris and my mother, who have never met, to join me. The three of us, plus my brother, Seamus, and his latest girlfriend, Tiffany Number Seven, are having a celebratory dinner. Harris is doing a segment for his show on Barry. We are hoping this will lead to a spin-off tentatively called *Rehab*. Barry's doctors have been very cooperative; two of them already have theatrical representation.

My mother is the first to arrive. She looks elegant in a navy sleeveless sheath dress, and proper heels. We watch the swans.

"When you stand here it is easy to believe nothing can ever go wrong," she comments. I wonder how much regret each day brings her. It is nothing she talks about.

Harris strides toward us. He is on. His posture is good, his movements confident. He is definitely poised. For what, we are not quite sure.

"There he is," I say to my mother.

"Oh, he looks Spanish," she says approvingly. "Very handsome."

"I don't think he's Spanish, Ma," I say.

"Stand up straight, and hold your stomach in, Maria," my mother warns in the last pressing moment before Harris is upon us. I can't hold my stomach in; there is standing room only in there. I remain silent.

Tiffany Number Seven is a sturdier version of Tiffanys One through Six. She works in the children's department of Polo, a step up from Saks lingerie from whence she hails. She was born to serve. She listens with enthusiasm and barely speaks. She is punctuated by her winks. My brother, who still really hasn't gotten over Tiffany Number Five, a smaller, smarter version of Number Seven, doesn't know what he has. But Harris does.

"I can't believe you know every episode," he clamors to an adoring Tiffany. "You must have missed *one*?"

"Nope. Not one," she responds, little charmer that she is. He is having a private conversation with old Number Seven, and the rest of us are watching.

Tiffany loves Harris's show. "Okay, what was your favorite episode?" he questions with pride.

Now my mother is getting jealous. In her day she could have wiped the floor with the likes of Number Seven and in her mind she is still there. Harris is definitely not playing this well. No wonder they moved him from news into reality programming. No political skills.

"Harris," my mother starts, fangs poised, "Maria tells me you used to live in Paris."

"Yes, in Le Marais," Harris says proudly.

"La Place des Voges is lovely," my mother says.

Harris is all puffed up. He is admired by Number Seven and can talk Paris with Ines.

"Are we going to order?" Seamus asks, losing his patience with the entire scene. "Maria, did you pick this bullshit place?"

"It's not as bad as some of her other picks," my mother chimes in.

Shot in the back by my coconspirator. I do not take the bait. I will take responsibility for the restaurant and the ill-mannered boyfriend.

"What's good here?" Harris asks. No one answers.

"So you lived in Paris when you used to be a journalist?" my mother inquires.

Harris twitches. He didn't see it coming. Shouldn't have flirted with Tiffany. Number Seven winks again in his direction. Harris smiles. He is just asking for it. Does he not understand the game?

"Nothing is good here, dude," my brother finally answers to a question long forgotten. "It's just expensive."

The network has put Harris up at Shutters, which I imagine makes him even more attractive to Number Seven. But alas he is mine. And so Harris and I depart the happy meal for Santa Monica and room service.

"Your family is great," Harris lies.

"Thanks," I say. Why bother apologizing for my own secret weapon?

The room at Shutters is white and blue and fluffy. The ocean view is illuminated by rides on the Santa Monica Pier. Harris has ordered steak and pommes frites for our second dinner.

"This is fabulous, H.," I say as I taste the perfectly prepared filet. "I am always famished after a bout with my family," I continue as a tender piece of meat practically melts in my mouth.

"What do you mean?" questions Harris.

"Well, you know, families, they make you crazy," I say, giving it little thought, and clearly not gauging the import of my words.

"My parents got divorced when I was five," Harris reminds me. "I don't really have a family."

"Sure, you do. You have a mother and a father," I blithely continue.

"But I can't remember ever seeing them in the same room," he says.

I look over, and Harris appears to have gotten smaller. It is clear this family stuff is a point of vulnerability.

"Well, you turned out great," I say, attempting to make it better, but only making it worse.

"I was raised by wolves," the shrunken Harris says, trying to lighten it up. But in a quick moment an essential piece of the puzzle has been revealed. When you think you come from nowhere all you have is the manufactured self. I know this because I live it. Maybe it is not so surprising that Harris and I have found each other.

Harris is sound asleep. Lost somewhere deep inside his heavy breathing. And I am left alone to think of my own fractured family, and to long for Harris's family, the one he never really had. Maybe we can make our own. I hope we can.

JUNE 13 Malibu Rehab is all we had hoped, a Spanish hacienda on Malibu Colony Beach. Is this any way to treat a drug addict? You bet it is. Barry and his primary physician can be found on the putting green in the atrium area, a trim young woman informs us. Harris, the crew, and myself head through the long Spanish-tiled living room into an enclosed outdoor area where Barry, decked out in knickers, a cashmere vest, and proper golf shoes, is practicing his short game with his young tan physician.

"I am Dr. Bob," the young man whispers as Barry sinks one. "Good shot, Bar."

"Let's get this," an agitated Harris barks at his crew. Harris at work is less pleasant than Harris at home. Maybe the ignoring thing isn't so bad after all.

"Hey, Bar," I say as they set up the shot. Nothing like spontaneity. Harris continues to bark in the background. "Okay can we get this?"

"Hey, old girl," Barry says. He is thin and his wan smile indicates that things are not as rosy as Barry and Dr. Bob are making out for the camera and crew.

"How are you doing?" I ask.

"I'd rather not complain," Barry replies.

"Ah, come on," I say. "I'm your agent."

"Things are just peachy," Barry says with very little irony.

And then the show begins. Once everything is set up for the Reality guys Barry and the doctor are back to demonstrating that rehab really is just a lot of yucks.

The chipper detainee looks beaten between takes, but the great thing about show people is that light. They can be at fucking death's door and then the curtain goes up or the light on the camera flashes red or an audience shows up and all of that becomes moot. They sparkle at their core.

Barry may be crazy, but he's definitely hooked in to the magic. And so his tired and sick body, hungry for its poisons, recedes and the light shines through for Harris and his entire reality crew. Barry and Dr. Bob sing a duet at the piano. Barry does performance art regarding sobriety. Barry refuses Harris's off-camera questions about his high-speed chase: "On the advice of counsel, old boy."

"When did you last see your wife?" Harris, still off camera, demands.

"Since before I left the U.K.," answers Barry, a flash of sadness darkening his painted-on glow.

"I see," remarks Harris. And then in true television, a sultry auburn-haired beauty roams into frame.

"Darling," gasps Barry.

"Hello, darling," the auburn beauty answers back with moist lips. This is definitely not the stout wife I imagined.

"Yvonne, everybody. Everybody, Yvonne." He continues formally introducing The Missus.

"Beautiful," squeals Harris. "Let's take it outside."

Barry and Yvonne stand next to the piano in a long embrace.

"Shit," grumbles Harris. "I wish we had gotten the hugging."

I say nothing, wishing Harris would shut up, embarrassed to be witnessing the "reality" of old Barry and Yvonne.

"How old do you think Yvonne is?" Harris asks me as we march out onto the sand.

"I don't know, thirty?" I say.

"Nope, twenty-three," Harris says with awe. "How old is that guy anyway?"

"In his forties," I say, knowing full well Barry will be sixty in a month.

"Wow," says Harris with even more awe. Ouch. Baby Harris and I felt that one. So why don't you find your own twenty-three-year-old? You little sack of . . .

Once the filming is complete, Dr. Bob insists that Harris and I come back for rehab dinner. And so we head over to Cross Creek (some shops in a parking lot in Malibu) to kill a couple of hours. As I sit on a bench watching some kids play in the little playground I wonder what Harris and I are doing. I may not be a teenage pregnancy, but almost. Irresponsibility can occur at any age.

I watch as Harris waits on line for an espresso. His darkness shines in the California light. I remember pursuing him in the snow. And then a wave of love. Perhaps the little Irishman is right and Harris remains unsure, but I am in love. I have to believe it counts. Everyone who thinks that they can make a loving family, cross this line—Maria O'Mara, not so fast.

"The espresso here is pretty good," Harris says and smiles, then takes a swig.

"Smells great," I say longingly.

"You've really been so good about the diet thing," Harris comments.

"My body has been rented by someone else, and he doesn't like coffee. What can I do?" I say.

Harris flashes his winning smile and pulls me toward him. "You're the greatest," he whispers.

I am home in Los Angeles being kissed by my New York beau. Look at me. I wish I could just stand here forever.

The dinner includes a well-known actress circa thirty, Barry, Yvonne, Harris, Dr. Bob, and me. The actress girl is very agitated. A symphony of unchoreographed movement, feet stomping, finger tapping, head turning, hair twisting, one two three, four. And feet stomping, finger tapping . . . If I watch her any longer I am going to be sick. I pick a point on the wall behind her head and try to stay focused. Definitely a drug casualty.

Barry leans over to pass the broccoli. "An antioxidant, my dear?" he offers.

"I think I'd rather have an antidepressant," I remark.

Barry and Yvonne have that warm pink glow. Surely the result of superb lovemaking. Yvonne smiles in Barry's direction and layers of his prickliness appear to fall away.

"Is that Daddy Warbucks?" Barry inquires in a whisper.

"The one and only," I whisper back. Barry looks back and forth at Harris and then at me. The director trying to make sense of the two characters.

"You really want him?" he asks.

"Yes," I say honestly, straining to hide the lilt of desperation.

Dr. Bob has dropped every name in all four editions of the Creative Directory. Actors, Directors, Producers, Above the Line, Below the Line—if they've been addicted (and according to him they all have) he has successfully treated them. So much for doctor/patient confidentiality. Barry and Yvonne have definitely not become Moonies. As for Actress Girl she'll be dating Dr. Bob before the end of dinner. It appears a true love connection is being made.

And then Barry sets out to claim Harris for me. If Barry's manipulations are successful, I should be happily married before dessert.

"Harris, are you the chap who does all of that fabulous trekking?"

"No—marathon running," Harris proudly corrects him. Watch it, Harris.

"Oh, that must be another friend of Maria's," Barry continues. Harris shoots me a look.

And then Yvonne gets into the act. "Darling," she chides, "don't mention her other beaus."

Harris is startled. He's been hit by a poison dart, and can't quite believe the sting. Never mind the toxicity.

"Well, I've done some trekking in Nepal," Harris attempts, trying to rehabilitate his image.

Yvonne and Barry smile at each other. They've got him.

"On holiday?" Barry asks in condescending tones. Harris nods. He is beaten. And then they go in for the kill.

"Maria has so many interesting friends," says Yvonne, whom I have never met before.

"Well, certainly a lot of chaps after her," comments Barry. I watch Harris's face fall.

"I've been trekking in New Zealand," Actress Girl pipes up. "We were shooting a film down there."

"Really?" asks Dr. Bob. He's all ears where Actress Girl is concerned. Although she is no longer recognizable, I am sure once she dries out and puts on thirty pounds she'll look just great. And by the way Dr. Bob is ogling her it seems he thinks so too. A doctor with an imagination, I like that.

"Well, Maria and I have an early plane to catch," announces Harris. He has had enough of the show. Although it was a surprise attack, my Harris has assessed the situation and he is getting out.

"Thank you for the dinner," I say with a wink. Barry stands up and throws his arms around me. I hold on just a little too long. "I'll call you tomorrow," I say.

"Yes," he says, patting my stomach. I am so touched by Barry's empathy I feel as if I might lose my shit in Malibu Rehab. Nothing Dr. Bob has not seen before. Nothing he couldn't handle at the rate of twenty G's per week.

It is a long twenty-minute ride from Malibu Colony south to our Santa Monica hotel. We do not speak. Harris is blasting the news on the car radio at full volume. Static crowds the airwaves. And then finally: "You're not seeing other people, are you?"

"Harris, I am pregnant, I have a very time-consuming job, and I love you," I say.

No response, just car radio static, and the *whirr* of the engine. How can two people who know each other so little contemplate a life together?

I see my moment, but I don't know how to seize it. It seems as if every woman who has ever lived and loved would know what to do now, but somehow I am lost. I need Harris. If I profess my love again he may spook. If I confront him on the issue of us I may risk losing us. How can I do that to Baby Harris? Who is this man who listens to static, and runs marathons, and can't say he loves me?

And then all of a sudden I am feeling really ill. My hands are covered in sweat. Why my hands?

"Harris, pull over," I screech. And then I am dousing the Pacific Coast Highway with our rehab dinner. I peer down into the gutter, and wonder how much longer Harris and I can go on misconnecting.

JUNE 14 It feels good to breathe the humid New York air. It's raining. There is a cab line. "I thought we were going to get a car," screams Harris into his cell. "More cutbacks?" he stammers incredulously.

I push our bags forward with all of my might. They move incrementally. I am fantasizing about getting home, making French toast, and going to bed. Sleep is my greatest refuge. Harris keeps making calls, refusing to accept his lot, stuck in a long cab line in the rain at Kennedy with me. And then I see our shot. A big Russian with a placard, walking out of the terminal in defeat.

I leap out of line. "Hey, mister, want a fare to Manhattan?"

"Okay," he says, still somewhat dejected.

"Great," I say. I try and get Harris's attention, but he is too engrossed in his cell call. Ah, whatever. I run back to the line, all the while watching the Russian to make sure he doesn't leave without us.

"Come on. I found a car," I say, pulling on Harris's leather jacket. Don't pull the material, his glance seems to say. So much contempt packed into such a small look. Amazing. Harris speeds into action, carrying all of the bags, making terrific use of his muscular runner's legs. Relieved to have been removed from the stratum of society that waits. A stratum he wishes to distance himself from, mostly because of its familiarity.

The two of us pile into the pristine black town car. The Russian glides us out of the airport with ease. There is quiet. The hush of money. Harris and I melt into the back seat. I am so tired. I am surprised and pleased when Harris takes my hand in his. He is gentle and strong in this moment. I feel glad I got him his car. He likes being chauffeured. I take note.

"Maria, will you marry me?" he says as easily as please pass the butter.

I think I feel a strong internal thrust from Baby Harris. Okay, okay. "Yes," I say, unable to contain a smile. And then the softest warmest most enveloping kiss. And it seems I practically have a life.

JUNE 17 I rush down Seventh Avenue on my way to the office. I am back in the city. The race is on; I am jostled and slammed. I am getting married. It feels frightening and tenuous. Is this how everyone feels? Actually it has been several days and Harris has not mentioned the marriage thing again. Not once. Is this a secret too? I try to find a locked compartment for these worries. I exist in a zone with just the right amount of denial and fight to keep going forward. Maybe the reason Harris runs marathons is to remind himself of the necessity of forward motion. I'm still attempting to wrap my brain around Harris. Maybe I should just love him and forget about understanding him. I enter my office building with the throngs of other workers.

I get off the elevator, and take a deep breath. I plan to go full throttle until they throw me out. I picture two guards carrying me back down to the street desk and all. Jed is on the phone.

"What about the lattes?" I mouth.

He puts up a finger signifying one minute. I stroll down the hall not yet ready to man my station. What I see scares me. Men and women attached to telephone lines by headsets, screaming, pleading, and cajoling. Searching for, owning, or seizing the power. The difference between show business and other businesses is that in show business they're just as glad to stab you in the front, says my colleague Sean, who suggested I pay through the nose for a clearing and a blessing or whatever that was I got for four hundred bucks. I notice him slinking in at ten something wearing dark glasses.

"Hard night?" I ask.

"Killer breakfast," he says. "I just got fired by my biggest client." And then I see the tears streaming down around his dark glasses.

"She'll be back," I try encouragingly.

"Not this time," he says. "She's become a Scientologist."

It's tough when the commodity you are trying to sell has a mind of its own. And big movie stars like the client he just lost run the show, until they don't. And when they don't, it is all over, and there is no one left to cater to their unreasonableness. It is such a ridiculous game chasing ephemeral power, everyone trying to take credit for the few successes and distancing themselves from the many failures. For many it is difficult to keep one's bearings, and then there are the few who find a winning mode of operation, and tenaciously hang in there and score. It is exhausting. But at this moment I feel I have no choice. A wave of anxiety and fear rises up in me. I am determined to fight for the little piece of the pie I have amassed. I am now officially in overdrive. I go back to my office to make a list.

Things to Accomplish

1. Marry Harris
2. Sign a major client
3. Solve serious social issues
   a) World hunger
   b) End all war
   c) Illiteracy
   d) Save the environment
4. Renew my agency contract

I plan to concentrate on items #1, 2, and 4. Although #3 would certainly take me to another level, i.e., personal fulfillment and Nobel laureate status, item #3 will still have to wait.

"Harris on line one," Jed calls out. My fiancé. I dare not speak the word.

"Hey," I say, trying for insouciance. Wishing we could run to City Hall right this minute.

"Could you pick me up some button-down shirts?" he asks. He cannot know how much such a request means to me. I am going shopping for my almost husband.

"Sure," I say, still trying for carefree. "What do you want for dinner?" I continue, figuring we're on a domestic roll.

"Uh, I have to work late," he says.

So I can make a late dinner. "Oh," I say, attempting to go with the program. Shirts, but no dinner. Does that mean something? "Any particular place you get your shirts?" I ask.

"Not really, try Barney's. I'll call you later," he says.

"Yeah, bye," I say. And then he is gone. And somehow I have managed a broken heart. And then God makes it up to me.

"The staff meeting has been postponed, and your lunch just canceled," Jed informs me. Hallelujah.

It is one of those perfect New York days. Each building is delineated by glistening sky. I head toward Barney's via Central Park South and decide to take Baby Harris for a small stroll in the park. I will make my life work out by sheer force of will. Everything is as it should be even if it is a forced fit. If the girl that came before Cinderella had just tried a little harder to get that shoe on she'd have been Mrs. Prince Charming.

Who can be sad in Barney's? With a flash of a charge card all this can be yours. Of course, it is not Bergdorf's. It is more faux nouveau, definitely more Harris. I buy the shirts with gusto, only throwing in the word *fiancé* a cool thirty-seven times. I wonder if the salesperson, I think he was a man, noticed me spit for good luck after each utterance: "My *fiancé*"—spit—"will love these," I say. Always spit for good luck.

I check out the deconstructivist designer ware, the toys for the child who already possesses everything in FAO Schwarz's current line, the semi-expensive semiprecious jewelry, and the most unattractive yet pricey handbags known to man. Now what? Don't make me go back to that rat-infested maze and put on a headset. And don't even think of sitting me in front of the high-definition screen in which we beam up London and the West Coast simultaneously so we can all laboriously read aloud open writing assignments at the major studios. Those assignments remain open for a reason. It could drive a person to drink. And don't you start either, Baby Harris. I know, no booze. Are you always going to be such a stickler?

I decide to take myself to lunch at Barney's chic restaurant.

It's in the basement, but God knows we don't mention that. "I'll have the thing with the arugula and goat cheese," I say without looking at the menu. My tone is semi-officious. The waiter scurries. If they didn't have a thing with goat cheese and arugula before, they do now. It will be well presented and at my table, pronto.

I peruse my luncheon compatriots. Charlie Rose and Amanda Burden. A lot of pencil-thin thirty-somethings who have forgotten their identities, and a vaguely familiar-looking Asian man perusing the menu. Who is that guy?

The arugula thing turns out to be a green salad with a few arugula leaves and a tiny piece of goat cheese. I inhale it and am still starving. I watch as the Asian guy orders one entrée, eats some of it, and then calls the waiter over and orders an entirely new meal. He retains the first plate of food, but doesn't seem to be eating it. I strain to see what it is. Baby Harris is campaigning. I wonder what else this guy has ordered.

Then I remember. He is from China. He is a major action director. I must sign him immediately. I develop a strategy en route to his table. I will drag him back to the office and sign him up right in front of the brass. If that doesn't impress them then at least I will die knowing that I tried as hard as anyone possibly could.

"Hello," I say, sort of hovering. The Chinese director stares at me warily. I remind myself I am in overdrive. There is nothing I will not do to make my life work. Nothing. I pull out the opposing chair. I sit down. "You are a superb director." I enunciate slowly and clearly, not really sure how good his English is, although they do hand him one hundred million dollars to make a movie. Maybe they use translators.

"You actwess?" he asks suspiciously.

"No, I am an agent," I say, still carefully articulating.

"That worse," he says as he commences entrée number two. Perhaps he thinks that if he ignores me I will go away. No way.

"I want to sign you," I say, delighted with my own directness.

"You crazy," he says, never looking up from his plate of food. Rapidly gliding food into his mouth with the not so familiar utensils.

"Yes, I am crazy and fearless," I say. "Great attributes for your agent."

"Go away," he says abruptly.

"No," I say. "Come to my office, meet my colleagues. Let us work for you. We will make you a happy man."

"You want me to call police?" he says in a disinterested manner.

"I'd rather have a bite of your chicken," I say.

"Okay, I don't like anyway," he says as he slides over his first plate. I am making headway, and I am having a second lunch. I finish off his chicken.

"Now you go away," he demands.

"No, now you come to my office," I demand back.

"You too crazy," he shrieks. Some of the pencil-thins look over. I do a finger flitter wave in their direction.

"No, I am just crazy enough," I say with a smile.

The Chinese director leans back in his chair and laughs. "How long you been agent?" he asks.

And so I drag my big Chinese fish up Fifth Avenue and across to the office entrance on West Fifty-fourth Street and call an impromptu signing meeting. "Is this the Chinese director who does the heartfelt, but edgy family dramas or the big blow-'em-up, technically superb action thrillers?" The Radical

Theatre Agent whispers to me as he glides into the conference room.

"That would be the latter," I whisper back.

The Radical Theatre Agent thinks for a moment and then points his right index finger at me in the universal sign for gun, signifying I believe, the action genre. I nod supportively.

"We are very glad to have you here," The Radical Theatre Agent begins in the same slow, well-enunciated quasi-foreign-speak I have been using with our honored guest.

"I know Engrish," the director informs us. I am sure he is wondering how it is just a few moments before he was having two entrées in the basement of Barney's, and now suddenly this.

"Of course," continues The Radical Theatre Agent. "The point is we love your work. We believe we can serve you well, and—"

"How you serve me?" the director asks.

"Well, in structuring deals—"

"The nice rittle girrl. Aggressive. She find me and bring me here," the director begins. "But I got more money I can ever spend. I happy man. I make my movies. I travel. You tell me you can make my work rife rast ronger" (work life last longer) "—that make me happy. But how can you do that? I make hit. I make another movie. I make too many bombs. I no work. What you can do about it?"

The director has spoken. The Radical Theatre Agent is stung. He looks at me with a combination of hate and rage. He left his office for this?

"The man you are speaking with possesses genius where material is concerned," I interject. "You would have a worldwide team sensitive to your needs who know and represent first-rate literary material. There are no guarantees, but one should be as well equipped as possible." I am speaking with no internal literary sense, but I am hoping the subtext is clear. Please, Mr. Big Chinese Fish, save my scrawny little ass. Don't make waves.

"I think about it," says the director, a little too attuned to the room's air of desperation. The director winces and abruptly gets up from his chair. "I got to go now," he explains.

We all jump up. Each of the twelve agents in the room shakes his hand. The meeting is over.

I make the long walk back to my office alone. Jumping off the balcony of my apartment would definitely do the job, but so messy. There must be a cleaner way.

"How'd it go?" Jed inquires.

I do the thumbs-down thing.

"Shit," says Jed. Never a good sign when our boy from Connecticut starts to swear.

I am back at my desk. No points for trying. Now whom can I call?

"Jed, bring me our list of famous people," I demand. Always the possibility you could hit a celebrity on a bad day. The wife leaves 'em, maybe they get a new agent. The car gets totaled, perhaps the day for a new agent. The mistress leaves, definitely the day for a new agent. I scan the list for known adulterers.

"Great meeting," The Radical Theatre Agent comments with no irony as he strides into my office. Are these fucking people totally insane? The worse things are, the more positive their appraisal. Do they think that their lies will erase their mishaps? Or are they consummate salespeople, just demented enough to believe that as long as they are selling it is all good?

My words have taken the express line from my heart to the tip of my tongue. I want to tell him I think that we are ever so fucked, and that the meeting went very badly. There is a war waging inside me. Truth versus survival. Survival versus truth. I try a wan smile as I bite a hole in my lip.

"So?" he presses. And then I get it. I am supposed to tell him he was great. He is an actor. He has just performed. He has publicly defecated. Posthumiliation there is no sense of self. There is just that feeling.

"You were brilliant," I begin. "You established a real rapport with him."

"You think so?" The Radical Theatre Agent asks.

"Definitely," I say.

"Well, good work getting him here," he says as he struts out of my office with his self-image intact. You do get points for trying, just not directly.

JUNE 20 I am stirring the risotto for our dinner. Harris likes it just so, and I am trying very hard at so.

"What do you think of this?" he asks, showing me a shirt and some slacks and a truly ridiculous tie. Too Vegas, but how can I tell him?

"It's great, but not so Maine," I say.

"You don't think so?" he says, his crest careening. It is beginning to occur to me that Harris is in a constant state of uncertainty. No sense of self, yet eager to fit in. It is a tough combination. The more I love him the more my heart aches for him. I can't let him show up at Mr. Social Register's looking like a mobster. They'll kill him. Well, actually they'll just ignore him, but that will kill him.

"I don't want to look like a Boy Scout," he says, demonstrating a certain level of frustration.

"Oh, right," I say, but that is the gig. I wonder if he will ever figure it out.

JUNE 21 We are dancing on the crackling hot sidewalk waiting for a cab. I am fat. I want to stop people on the street and explain. I am not really fat, just pregnant. It is not allowed. And so I must go cowlike to Maine to the Social Registers' while Harris tries his luck at climbing up the social rungs.

Two planes and five states later we are in Bar Harbor. Social Hopefuls waiting to be remembered in a small Maine airport. Three hours later, "You the Schwartmans?" a tall fifty-something fellow asks.

"More or less," I say.

Harris twitches uncomfortably at my response. Each word will be weighed. Every moment scrutinized. If we play this correctly we may be transformed from socially hopeful to socially viable. I want to grab his hand and run. You will never be tall and white. Who cares? But for Harris acceptance is paramount, especially from this dying legacy.

"Just throw your stuff in the back of old Stella," directs the tall stranger.

"Thank you." I smile as I lob my suitcase into the back of the oldest red pickup in the continental United States.

"You're entirely welcome." The tall stranger twinkles. "I am Charlie," he says.

I offer my hand. "Maria O'Mara. Nice to meet you."

Harris winces.

"I guess we're meant to jump in the cab with Charlie," I say. "Who is Charlie?" I whisper.

"Their man," Harris answers with an air of condescension.

Whatever. Charlie I like. Harris on the other hand . . .

We ride along in silence, and then a loud thumping jolts me from my reverie. It is a vigorous pounding. I search for the source. Ah-ha. An expectant Harris cannot control himself. His leg is having a jig right up against the seat of the old truck. Hey, buddy, watch the material, would ya? I glance over at Charlie. His eyes smile. He gives the faintest of shrugs: what the hell? I flash a smile. Harris remains oblivious.

We turn onto a gravel path that leads us to a large white clapboard house made less austere by a friendly red door. I inhale the cool Maine air. It feels restful here. This might not be so bad. I wish Harris would submit to the surroundings, but he is New York City wound. Ready to make his move. A man with a plan.

"Well, here you go," says Charlie as he gets out of the truck and unloads our bags. "Good luck," he says as he jumps back into the truck.

"Thanks," I say as Harris runs on ahead to the bright red

door. The knocker resounds as he beseeches the Social Registers to let him in. He has been campaigning for this invitation for months. His excitement is palpable.

A tall pleasant-looking woman in her thirties comes to the door. Her dirty-blonde hair is cut short. She wears very clean faded blue jeans and a crisp white button-down shirt and navy clogs.

"May I help you?" she asks, unsure of who or what she is dealing with.

"You must be Maisie," Harris commences in his obsequious tones.

This is more than I can bear. It is definitely time to tune out. Maisie seems to have some vague recollection of yet another two houseguests.

"I guess you'll fit in one of the third-floor bedrooms," she continues with less than enthusiastic diplomacy.

"Great," agrees chipper old Harris, as Maisie Social Register leads us up steep stairs.

"Jack and the others are out in the boat," she explains. I guess Mr. Social Register is called Jack.

"Mom," cries a kid from outside.

"Coming," cries Maisie. "I am sure you'll find everything you'll need," Maisie adds as she leads us into an attic room with two single beds, a sink, and a slanted ceiling. She smiles as best she can and makes a hasty retreat.

Harris grins. "Isn't it great? So New England," he says.

It ain't Bali, that's for sure. I smile and nod. The less said the better. It's only three days. And then I can go back to the city, and my imploding life. I don't want to be projected into some other world, but Harris does. Beam him up, Scotty. He's heading into the third dimension and refuses to return until he is a full-fledged Yankee. As if this were a viable alternative. "Whatever," I say aloud.

"What?" asks Harris.

"Oh, nothing. Just talking to myself," I say.

"I hate it when you do that," he snaps.

"Got it," I say. Another demerit. At this rate I'll never become an Eagle Scout. It's only three days.

"Cocktails are in the backyard," Maisie directs as she rushes into the kitchen to get/do something. I can see she is one of those women who is always very busy. I head out that way and am delighted by the physical surroundings. The "yard" is a large expanse of gently sloping lawn, which leads down to the water. The coast is rocky and well defined. There is nothing gentle or sandy or Southern California about it. And it is cold, well, sixty-five degrees.

The guests too are more austere than those of Malibu or the Hamptons. This is a no-nonsense, high-achievement crowd. Very proper and on the precipice of getting hammered. I am poised for the next scene. I wonder if I'll even be able to tell the difference between their sober and inebriated states.

Mr. Social Register is recapping his day's sailing adventures for his guests—many of whom were on the friggin' boat. It reminds me of women who scrutinize pictures of their newborns while the gurgling baby is nestled in their arms. Is it more real in the photographs? Or in this case the retelling? I am jarred from my thoughts by a too shrill laugh. It is Harris. Standing too close. Laughing too loud. What is he hoping to achieve? Does he think that some of Mr. Social Register will actually rub off? That he'll become a taller more refined version of himself?

These people seem perfectly fine. Lawyers, financial types, pretty enough wives; most of them have known each other since childhood. They live by prescribed "To Do's." This is what they "Do" in the summer. The question persists: what are Harris, Baby Harris, and myself doing here? This is certainly not a workable crowd by my standards. I laugh to myself as I realize I couldn't get any farther away from Hollywood and still be in the continental United States. I long for my own gin and tonic, but Baby Harris is having none of that. So I stand alone waiting to see what will happen next. Perhaps I can compute the hours until we get the hell out of Dodge. That will engage some of the next ten minutes at least. It's now a little less than three days.

"Dinner is called for at eight," announces Maisie. "We'll be heading next door," she says and smiles. This girl is an expert at speaking to the middle distance. And she has excellent posture. I am betting Miss Porter's. Harris can't wait to head out on the boat tomorrow morning. Yachting, you know. My feet hurt. And I have this feeling that I am being pushed down physically by some invisible force. It is taking all of my energy to just maintain.

"Do you sail, Martha?" Mr. Social Register asks me.

"A bit," I say. I suppose Martha is as good a name as any for me. And then the entire cocktail party, twelve adults and seven children, head next door.

We walk down the street and up yet another craggy Maine road straight into the Gilded Age. Harris pumps out his chest, readying himself for the next phase of his performance. The proportions of this house are absurd. Our crowd barely makes a dent as we stand in the foyer waiting.

And then Wyatt James sweeps in to greet her guests. She gives Mr. and Mrs. Social Register the big hello, and then assesses the crowd.

"Maria!" She smiles. And suddenly the spotlight is on me. How does she know her? Everyone is wondering. Harris is shot. He slumps over in semidefeat. This is not my show. This is his climb. I am the necessary but unwanted baggage.

"Hey," I say, a noncommittal salutation. Praying for this moment to end, gathering that Wyatt now summers in Maine, but of course. "You remember Harris," I continue.

Wyatt waits just a beat too long. It is clear she doesn't. "Of course," she says, smiling, then quickly turning her attention to Martin and their middle son, Edgar, who are attempting to usher everyone into the backyard.

Edgar, the coolest nine-year-old I know, grabs my hand. "Who's that guy?" he asks, pointing his chin in Harris's direction.

"Your competition," I answer.

"Impossible," he says, looking directly at Harris. Shot again. They take aim young here. Oh, well, social climbing is an extreme sport. Only the toughest survive. I hold on tightly to the hand of my little compatriot, grateful for this respite and the knowledge that it is only three days.

In true Wyatt style everyone has a huge lobster to tackle. Fin, who showed up late and who is apparently staying with us at the Social Registers', is busy pumping Harris back up. A deflated balloon is better with all of the air out. The three James progeny, Edgar, John, and Michael (our young hosts), have taken an instant dislike to Harris and are pelting him with straw wrappers and bits of soggy napkin laden with lobster entrails. Baby Harris does not seem to be enjoying lobster one bit. So now in addition to feeling an overwhelming weight pushing down on me, I am seasick. I can't wait for sailing.

"Oh, fantastic!" screams Harris across the table to Mr. Social Register, who has the look of one who has been assaulted. It is a look he wears every time Harris speaks to him. Lose some octaves, buddy. As Harris continues Wyatt winces. She is working that side of the street. She climbed up here one rung at a time and is in no need of a sidekick, but Harris remains clueless. After all, Fin is enjoying Harris's company and they are here with the rich and the socially prominent. What could be better?

And then they are all sloshed. Their faces have turned to wax. Something you do not notice when you too are drinking but is ever apparent when you are not. And again the crowd, which now measures forty plus, is on the move. We are going barn dancing at yet another estate. I walk along in the dark alone, slightly removed from the crowd, breathing in the cold moist air, hoping that my nausea will recede.

"Have you seen Harris do the Professor?" asks Fin. His singsongy brogue is not doing a thing for my seasickness.

"No," I say curtly, hoping he will move on.

"Oh, he's fabulous when he's performin'," he cries. "You'll love it." I bet.

A live band blares. Edgar and I dance. Together in the beat, but in our own worlds. What do nine-year-olds fantasize about? Forty-year-old pregnant women pray for sea legs and promise

God that they will do charitable works if he lets them get through the evening without booting. Or so I've heard. I am riding the waves of my nausea, cold and sweaty, a marvelous combination. And then Harris grabs the mike. Uh-oh.

"I would just like to thank Maisie and Jack for having us up here and am pleased to introduce, all the way from New York City, The Professor," Harris shouts. He turns his back to the crowd for a few moments' worth of rearranging, and then he turns back. His face is transformed. He wears a pair of black horn-rimmed glasses upside down, and he has tied a sweater around his neck. He looks almost Asian. I am not sure I get the look he is going for. He signals the band. They begin playing a raplike tune. And he is off. Rapping about The Professor's origins ". . . all the way from New York Citay . . ." and periodically engaging in some not bad break dancing. The crowd claps along rhythmically. Do they somehow think that this is more politically correct than having an actual African American perform? Or was P. Diddy booked?

The performance is interminable. No one here has the beat. I have got to get out. All attention is fixed on Harris. I want to shout *They're not laughing with you,* but Harris is fueled. He bathes in their alleged admiration. And just as I'm questioning the authenticity of their delight a brightly colored Lilly Pulitzer–clad creature with streaked blonde hair and a wide bum jumps up onto the stage. "Miss Lilly" and Harris prance stylishly in a manner that would make Mick Jagger proud. The crowd goes wild—they really do like him. I walk rapidly away from the barn.

Alone in the dark. Nothing out here can be more frightening than the scene I have just escaped. The air feels good, and for the first time since we have landed I feel free.

"Hello, young lady," says Charlie, who is also out for a stroll in the dark. He is wearing waders and carrying two flashlights.

"Going night fishing?" I ask.

"Nah, going over to the club to look for balls. Care to join me?" he asks.

"Sure," I say. We walk along silently in the dark, and it feels comfortable.

"Not bad," Charlie exclaims as I shake loose two golf balls from some thick bushes at the edge of the rough on the third hole. "Too bad I didn't bring an extra pair of waders. You seem to have a natural talent for this line of work."

"I knew I was good at something," I say, enjoying the praise.

Charlie has waded out into the pond. His search is aided by something that looks like a large strainer. "Now this is where you can make a killing," he explains. I wonder if he sells the balls or just uses them himself. "Heavy load here," he exclaims. "Run and get one of the buckets from the golf cart, would you?"

"Sure," I say, scurrying off. We're having fun now.

Next, Charlie and I jump into the golf cart and he barrels across the fairway full throttle. And then we barrel across the green again. We laugh uproariously. Badly behaved children delighting in our mischievous pursuit. We stop to catch our breath, and Charlie leans over and gently touches my face. I see fireflies everywhere. Airborne magic and then the moment is over. Did that just happen?

"Can't stand waste," says Charlie, referring to the legion of balls we have collected. He helps me out of the cart and we make our way back in the direction of the barn. Charlie disappears into the dark and I find my way back into the dispersing crowd, hoping that my absence will not have been noticed.

"Maria," cries Harris.

"Harris, you were great," I say. "Where did you learn—"

He cuts me off. "I've been looking for you. I was scared," he says.

"Just stepped out to get some air," I say. Golf ball hunting he would never understand.

"Are you okay?" he asks. Harris seems truly concerned.

"I am okay," I say as I loop my arm around his waist.

"Don't disappear like that," he says as he pulls me close. I am glad he is here. We walk along in silence. Maybe this is a vacation. "Fin is going to bunk with us," he interjects.

"Okay," I say, feeling the warmth of his body.

It is a tight fit. Harris, Baby Harris, and me in one single bed, and Fin in the other.

"Can you move your knee?" Harris winces.

"Oh, sorry," I say, trying to figure out how we can reasonably fit here. Fin has fallen fast asleep and is snoring loudly.

"Maria, you have got to get your elbow out of my neck," Harris instructs.

"I'm working on that," I respond. How long are we going to contort ourselves to feign membership here?

JUNE 22 Mr. Social Register's sailboat is magnificent. Harris is an eager crewman. Spinnaker to you too, buddy. Baby Harris is not amused. There is no way I can stave off my nausea.

"How long have you and Harris been married?" Maisie asks as I puke my guts out over the side.

"Oh, we're not yet," I say.

"That's modern," she retorts with a knowing smile. Now it is I who stare off into the middle distance. I am admitting to nothing.

"So you haven't gotten your sea legs just yet, eh?" comments Fin, who has joined Maisie in chronicling my illness. Why do they just keep standing there? Fortunately for Fin, snappy retorts are physically impossible at the moment. I could kill him. This morning when I awoke I was incapable of turning my head. Couldn't we have survived up here without him? Maybe he'll fall overboard. Of course I'd be too sick to call for help. The end of Finber O'Shaunessy. I am feeling better already. This short jaunt seems interminable.

And just when I think I couldn't possibly have anything more to give, I am sick again. "Just keep lookin' at the horizon, darlin'," comforts Fin, who has ever so kindly come aft to check on me. Hasn't he drowned yet? I try fantasizing harder. You have to believe to achieve.

As soon as we return to land Mr. Social Register, a.k.a. Captain Bly, informs us that croquet will be on the south lawn in thirty minutes.

"This is so great," comments Harris. What is great? The constant activity? The frenetic energy? The whiteness of it all?

We race back up to the third floor to take showers in what counts as a bathroom up here. Now I understand the term *water closet*. Fin has beaten us back and is singing away at the top of his lungs. "Oh, there once was a *bum, bum, bum* . . ."

"Leave some hot water," I scream a bit shrilly.

"Calm down, Maria," snaps Harris.

"Right," I say. Even I know I have crossed a line. I try deep yoga breathing as I wait in the hall not feeling quite magnanimous enough to leave this spot for fear some croquet rival will beat me into the shower. Slow deep breaths, I can handle this.

Harris and I head downstairs for this pre-cocktail activity. I am counting on it being a short game, considering it is all that stands between us and booze. Foiled. One must drink and play. Our host greets us with a pitcher of something frothy. He is dressed in madras shorts, an orange button-down shirt, navy and white polka-dot bow tie, and a beanie cap with a pinwheel attached.

"I've got to go change," whispers Harris the minute he catches sight of Mr. Social Register's getup.

"No, darling, only he goes down the rabbit hole," I try as reassuringly as possible. God, please spare Harris the humiliation of an attempt at emulating the host's sartorial statement.

"B-b-but—" Harris stammers like a four-year-old.

"Just the host goes goofy," I snap, desperately wishing to down about three of those alcoholic lemonades. I grab a mallet. When in Rome. At this point I am out for blood.

"I am red," I announce as I whack the living shit out of the little wooden ball. I am through several wickets, and out way ahead of the others who have hit more gingerly.

"Well done," comments Mr. Social Register, pitcher in hand, poised to pour. "Not drinking?" he says, wrinkling up his patrician nose in disapproval.

"Not today." I smile.

"Oh," he says and walks off.

But do have one on me, old boy.

Now someone's young redheaded nanny gets up to take a whack. How democratic. The men all leer as the only Brit in the crowd, and more importantly the only woman under twenty-five, nails it. Mr. Social Register goes bouncing over with the pitcher. He is all smiles.

"Well done, Beatrix." He smiles. She beams. If I were Maisie I'd get out the old shotgun about now. My heart is pounding. I am feeling that pulled-down feeling again, but I am intent upon beating the pants off little Miss B., and so I ignore what is beginning to register as pain, and continue to smash at the ball.

"Oh, I hit you," shouts the redheaded nanny with glee as my wooden ball rolls out to the hinterlands so far off course I may never get back. "So sorry," she screams as she wiggles on ahead under the watchful and approving eye of all of the men including Harris.

There it is again, a terrible, tearing sensation from somewhere deep inside me. It is now impossible to ignore.

"Is there a ladies' room in the boathouse?" I inquire of Mr. Social Register.

"Yes," he says.

I hobble off wincing discreetly or so I hope. There is something wrong here, but everything is moving slowly, and I can't seem to put the pieces together.

"Don't miss your shot," Harris calls.

"Right," I say. I walk over to my ball with my mallet still in hand and smash the fucker one more time. My ball hits several other balls including the now well-inebriated Nanny's. She wails. I am in a better position than I was, and then the pain is so searing I sit down exactly where I am.

"Is she drunk?" someone inquires. And then a group of people is huddled around me. They are all looking down at me and speaking, but I can't seem to hear their words. There is just pain in every direction.

"Go get my father-in-law," shouts Maisie, who now is crouched next to me. "How far along are you?" she asks.

I stare into her slightly freckled face. She has kind violet eyes, something I just noticed.

"Can you get up?" she asks.

I nod, and that is when I become aware of blood. The moisture I am sitting on may not be wet grass. There is blood on one of my legs. Two people help me up. And then Charlie appears.

"Hi," he says calmly. "I am going to fly you down to Boston."

Harris and Fin and I get into a big black BMW driven by Charlie.

"Are you a doctor, then?" Fin asks.

"Nah," Charlie answers curtly. "On the hospital's board."

I am audibly groaning.

"Maria," says Harris in admonishing tones.

Charlie drives us to a small airport, and right out onto the runway to an awaiting jet. "Everything is ready, sir," a handsome guy says to Charlie through the driver's-side window. And then there is concern as to my ability to walk up stairs, which I find ridiculous, until I falter.

Charlie is asking Harris questions about my pregnancy.

"He's in denial," I say, trying to explain the situation. Harris grimaces, but Fin is all ears.

"I thought you were only four weeks along," he says.

I thought it was a secret.

And then all of a sudden the pieces are fitting together.

"What's he doing here?" I demand from Harris as we are all belting ourselves into the jet.

"Well, he'll need a ride home," Harris explains.

"Take a bus," I shout at Fin. "Get him out of here," I scream.

"Maria, stop," says Harris.

"Out of here now," I scream.

Fin remains belted into his seat. "She's delirious," he says pertly in his tiresome brogue.

"I am not delirious," I say. It hurts. It hurts. "Please just let us have some privacy," I beg.

Harris hands me a pile of towels to sit on. Charlie and the pilot are forward. And we are airborne. I guess Charlie is their dad not their man. The dad with the jet who sits on boards. Now I am really wondering what it is he does with those golf balls.

It is all bad. Baby Harris isn't going to make it. And I am having an operation. And Harris is missing out on his weekend.

"Well, you got to ride on a private jet," I say to Harris as they wheel me away. "It hurts, so much," I say aloud to no one in particular.

"Oh, Maria," says Harris in put-upon tones. He has had it. I can't blow-job my way out of this one.

"How do you know Charlie?" the anesthesiologist asks me. Small talk before he takes me next door to death so his buddies can scoop out all that displeases them. All that was everything to me.

"He's a friend's father," I say.

"He's a great guy," the anesthesiologist continues. "Now, Maria, can you count backwards?"

I think of my own father, who was an anesthesiologist, and then of my mother. I want my mother.

"Ten, nine, eight . . .," I say before I float off the precipice to nothingness.

JUNE 23 I wake up in a big private room. Thank you, Charlie. There is a beautiful basket of flowers. I lean over and grab the card. Harris and I will make it. Nope, Wyatt sent them. I guess all of Maine that cares know about the messy miscarriage. That word. I feel as though I am rapidly descending in an elevator. The fright is overwhelming. And then I want to cry, but no tears come. I am in the bottom of a hole, and am too exhausted to climb out. I am alone in Boston. And there is no Baby Harris. I am truly alone. And then I hang on as I ride the rapid elevator down again. What is happening here? Where is my baby?

No one comes to visit or calls all night. Nurses run in and out just to make sure. Make sure of what? That I get no sleep whatsoever? That I never reach a state of unconsciousness where all of this reality floats away and I can feel whole again? I can't stop thinking of the four birth control pills I took two nights after Harris and I engaged in unprotected sex. Baby Harris knew

I would have offed him from the start and so he chose to leave. To get the hell out. He knew Harris didn't love me. He knew me from the inside out and he chose to leave.

"Hey there," says Fin all perky the next morning. The little leprechaun who will not die.

"Hey," says Harris, who saunters in a few paces behind. Less perky than his compatriot, but tan and rested nevertheless.

"Where did you guys stay last night?" I ask, truly curious.

"With Charlie up in Beverly," comments Harris, clearly wanting to skip over this point.

"Was it nice?" I ask, still curious.

"Fantastic," yodels the little leprechaun. He is so pleased with the turn of events he can barely stand it. "We went skeet shootin', and the cook prepared a lovely butterflied lamb."

"Charlie is a great host," says Harris in the hopes of shutting Fin up.

But old Fin is impervious. "The house—or should I say *estate*—has been in the family for generations," he continues.

"How do you feel?" asks Harris with a tinge of embarrassment.

"I feel okay," I say. "Ready to break out of this joint." This is the best tough-girl act I can muster. I am barely holding it together. I want to grab onto Harris. I want him to wrap me in a tight embrace while I scream as loud and as long as I can. I want to be alone with Harris and my grief.

"Anyway, Charlie said he'll be ready to take us down to Teterboro in an hour," informs Fin. Is he really this oblivious?

"Oh, we can't impose upon him for any more free jet rides, you guys," I say. "We'll just take the commuter flight back to La Guardia."

Both Fin and Harris look crushed. No more jet rides? Am I fucking crazy? They are not going to let this happen.

"Well, actually he has business in New York," starts Harris.

No, Harris, Charlie has manners and grace.

"I am sure he is just saying that," I begin, mortified by my little taker and his Irish sidekick.

"No, I am not," says Charlie, leaning on the inside of the doorjamb. He is smiling. He is tall and handsome in khakis and a blue button-down shirt. His eyes sparkle. And I feel safe. "Let's get you checked out," he says. "My pilot is already at the airport."

"I know you're lying," I say.

"You don't know shit," he says and laughs. It is surprising to hear him swear, and yet it does break the tension.

As I begin to put my clothes on I see that they are all bloodstained. Another quick ride in the elevator. I am careening down and I am panicked. I know it's not real, but still I am terrified. And then Harris walks in with my duffel bag.

"Where did this come from?" I ask.

"Fin packed for us when you were out on the lawn," he says. So there, Fin is a good guy is the subtext. Screw you, Harris. I am sick knowing he touched my things.

"Thanks," I say. I pull out some jeans and a sweater. "This is so hard," I say to Harris.

"I'll be waiting outside," he says as though I have said nothing. The elevator rides and his denial are just not working for me.

Another car and driver meet us on the tarmac at Teterboro. The boys, Charlie, and I ride in silence across the George Washington Bridge. The car slides up to my apartment building.

"Great building," says Charlie reassuringly. The driver jumps out and grabs my bag.

"Thank you so much for your help and kindness," I say to Charlie.

"Sure," he says. "Take care."

I get out of the car expecting Harris to follow. I turn, but there is no movement. He sits wedged in the car. There is no way he is leaving Fin alone in the car. No way he is going to miss out on one second of face time with the biggest fish he has ever encountered.

"I'll call you," says Harris. I nod a disbelieving nod as I head into the lobby.

"*Buenos tardes,* Miss Maria," says Freddie the doorman. "You no look so good. "You sick?"

"Nah, just tired," I say.

"Okay, you go rest," he says.

"Thanks, Freddie," I say as I secret myself away in the little teak elevator. I am so lonely and so glad to be back in the city and my own apartment. Maybe I can go to sleep and wake up and the last two days really will not have happened.

JUNE 25 It is 3 A.M., and I am up in the city that never sleeps. It sleeps. At least on the Upper West Side it does. I walk across the living room floor and plant myself in the window seat. Just me, the Hayden Planetarium, and the flashing light on my message machine:

"Maria, ah, this is Jed. The Grand Poo Bah is looking for you . . . ah, well, call in, would ya?" *Click*.

"Maria," says The Grand Poo Bah. "We've received word that you have been hospitalized. Ah, well, we do hope all goes well there. The point is Maria, that I am here to meet with you and unfortunately you're not here, so ah, unfortunately we will not be renewing your contract, but ah, we do wish you all the best and—" *Click*.

"Yes, Maria, Grand Poo Bah again. I believe we were cut off, but in any event we expect a four-week transition period and you and The Radical Theatre Agent will work out the details. Thank you. Jenna, are you still on the line? Get me Sherry Lansing, would you?"

"Okay," says Jenna, and then a flat dial tone, and I am over and out. No baby. No job. Just rushing to my death all alone in an imaginary elevator.

When I finally awaken it is 3 P.M. My bedroom is hot and sticky. One of those humid New York days. Jed's voice wafts through the apartment.

"Hey, are you there?" he almost pleads.

I can't really answer that question. I may be here physically. I am contemplating getting up and turning on the little window air conditioner, but it is too hard to move. I am too hot. And then I remember. And I am once again rapidly descending in an elevator to nowhere. It is all a fantasy except for the panic, which is as real as anything I have suffered. I wonder when Harris will surface. And then I decide to go out.

As I enter the subway station at Eighty-first Street and Central Park West a burst of warm air swirls around me. I think of Marilyn Monroe in *The Seven Year Itch*. Maybe if my mother had named me Bubbles everything would have turned out better. Finally the B train shows up. I dash into the cool car. A few dreary people, but plenty of room. And air-conditioned air. The cold feels good. I decide to ride to Brooklyn. Maybe there everything will look different. I think not, but I am holding on to the hope. I am praying for a change in perspective, even a slight one.

I get off the train in DUMBO. Down Under the Manhattan Bridge Overpass is a miasma which is Brooklyn Heights adjacent.

Earnest creative types living on the urban edge. I pace the commercially zoned streets looking for a future. If only I could extract the means to one from the steam rising up off the deserted streets. What I am hoping to find is not here and so I move on.

Then I am back among the clearly motivated. Prada shoes and big ideas, Brooklyn Heights is happening. I stand on the esplanade and take in the Brooklyn Bridge. Maybe I should adopt a new aesthetic. When you have suffered this much loss it is almost impossible to figure out how to stuff the hole.

I am afraid to feel and so I contemplate an apartment in Brooklyn. It will be spare and minimalist. I'll have a few artifacts, some from Asia and some from Mexico. Light will pour into my space off of the river. My thoughts will be clearer. I will grow herbs in window boxes. I will know what to do next. Finally I make myself stare across the river at Manhattan. I almost had everything I desire, but I blew it. Somehow I keep grabbing at air. I know this, but it is as though I don't have enough information to cross the finish line. How is it that they all keep moving ahead, and I am still just watching? Standing here dead in my tracks.

I get back on the subway and head back in the direction of my own life. I need to talk to Harris. Maybe it will still turn out all right.

"Maria," someone calls from the other end of the car. It is a film company executive, commonly known as a "D girl"—development girl—within the industry. Too tired for work. The young woman moves toward me. What to do now?

The train empties out at the West Village. What is her name?

"Hey," I say. Words are costly. I am functioning on a limited amount of energy.

"What are you doing?" the young woman asks.

Well, you see, I am riding the B train in search of a new life. No, I shouldn't say that. Not going to work. Having miscarriages. Getting fired. "I had to meet a filmmaker in Brooklyn," I finally say. Of course he's fiction, but that allows him to be young and an Academy Award winner, and a kind and generous person. A true invention.

"How are you?" she continues.

"Not great," I say. It is a bold answer. Agents are always great.

"Me neither," she says. "I just had a miscarriage."

Did she just say that? "Me too," I say.

"How far along were you?" she questions. The sisterhood.

"Four and a half months," I say.

"Oh, Gawd," she says. "I was only two and a half, and I am totally freaked. My husband just doesn't get it. Do you have a therapist?"

"No," I say. She hands me one's card and gets up at her stop.

"Feel better," she says, and she is gone.

I am overcome with emptiness. An old man snoozes at the other end of the car. Maybe he and I are the last two people on the planet. Maybe that D Girl was really a messenger from God. But what is the message? Go to a shrink?

JUNE 26 "Maria"—this is The Radical Theatre Agent calling. "I understand you have spoken to the Grand Poo Bah. Please contact me immediately. We must decide on a course of action with regard to your clients. Also please know that the Agency will support you in whatever story you want to tell regarding your termination." BEEP—he is cut off. What a swell fellow. But you see, the story is too long to tell.

"Ah, Maria, this is Harris." No shit. "Ah, we need to talk, so call me," he says, and then the dial tone. Uh-oh. The we-need-to-talk call. But what about denial? I'll keep your apartment key and we'll just keep going as if there is love and kindness and no ulterior social motives that impel you. How about that, motherfucker?

"Maria, it is your mother. I have a bad feeling. Is something wrong? I hope not. Call me." Good old Ines. How does she know? Because she is a mother. And I am not.

JUNE 27 Harris waits for me on a street corner. I am picking him up in a cab. We are on our way to a party.

"You look nice," he says.

I smile. This is the strangest uh-oh meeting. We do cocktails and then you dump me? Whatever. One foot in front of the other. I am focusing on acting normal. My heart is not broken. I do not reside inside an invisible elevator that keeps plunging me to depths heretofore unknown. I am sporting a new white dress from Polo. My hair has been properly coifed by Frederic. I am en route to a party. Things are great.

"Did you go to the office today?" Harris asks.

"Not yet," I say. He grimaces. "I'll go tomorrow," I promise. I have not told Harris that I have been sacked. I do not want to give him any ideas. If he finds out it is in vogue it might give him the courage to do it himself. I focus on how happy I must be because I am going to a party with the man I love. Da da da, I am singing in my brain.

The cab stops in front of the main branch of the New York Public Library. Good old Harris has scored again.

"A charity event?" I inquire.

"Yeah, a friend from work had the tickets, but couldn't attend," Harris explains. As we head up the library steps it smells expensive.

"Well, it's definitely not an environmental charity," I say as we step into a glistening ice castle. In one of the hottest weeks in the city's history ice sculptures abound.

"Maria," says Harris through gritted teeth.

"Okay," I say, intending to put a lid on it. All of the swells are here for one last bash before the summer season kicks in and they all leave town. Television talk show types and society doyennes parade designer gowns. It is an older, moneyed crowd.

Harris leaps into action. He downs as many crab claws and choice prawns as he is physically able. There ought to be a legal limit. Then when he is sated: "Maria, let's dance," he insists. Yes, of course, because we are so happy, da, da, da.

We enter the dance floor, but my feet betray me. They will under no circumstances be a party to da, da, da.

"What's the matter?" Harris finally asks.

Oh, the regular. No baby. No job. I hate party crashing. "I am not feeling all that well," I say.

His features go south. "You don't want to leave, do you?" he stammers. Now it is he who is fighting back rage. He didn't fucking spend his entire day scoring these tickets not to imbibe in the prime rib.

"Oh no," I say. I try for a smile, but apparently my lips have been speaking to my nondancing feet. They will not participate. Come on, I say to every part of myself. Don't you want to close?

You're nobody till somebody loves you. Remember? Da da da. I try and tap my foot to Peter Duchin and his lovely band. This is my last chance. There is the fucking finish line. Keep dancing, Maria.

It is a sit-down with designated seating. Harris leads me to my seat. My place card reads ROBIN POPEJOY.

"Who are the Popejoys?" I whisper to Harris before he sashays off to his place at the far reaches of the table.

"I don't know," he says.

"What?" I say.

"Some guy at work got these tickets from a friend of his roommate's," he explains.

How many generations of removal is that, I wonder as I plant myself between an old rich guy with yellow teeth and a bow tie, and some young stud. The stud is definitely a walker.

"Hello," I say to the stud. "Maria O'Mara."

"I am Ricky," he says in his high-pitched falsetto. Definitely a gay walker.

"So, Robin," begins the older gentleman, having done his homework and read my place card.

"Yes," I say with a smile. Why explain anything to anybody? I look across the table at Harris, who is laughing conspiratorially with his dinner companions. Now who exactly is this charade for?

We are back out on the library steps. The warm air feels good.

"Goodnight, Thomas," one of the dowagers calls across the steps to Harris. He smiles and waves.

"Jesus, Harris," I begin.

"What?" he says, perplexed.

"Now we can't even be ourselves," I shout.

"Maria, lower your voice."

"I don't want to," I shout.

Harris gently takes my elbow, and we proceed through the throngs of people onto the sidewalk, and around the corner to Bryant Park.

"I can't take this anymore," I scream. Harris sits down on a bench in the well-manicured park.

"Can't take what?" he demands.

"Riding the social escalator to nowhere," I shout. "Pretending that things are la-dee-dah when I am experiencing a broken heart!"

Harris just sits there. I feel a surge of anger. I am only just beginning.

"I don't feel well," I scream out, not certain that is entirely true. I mean, there are the elevator rides to the far reaches of hell and some residual spotting, but other than that I am really not so bad. "And now we go out incognito! We are no longer social hopefuls. We have leapt to the awesome category of social pretenders. We could probably be prosecuted for impersonating the Popejoys!"

"I just wanted to get you out. Have some fun," Harris says, looking truly hurt.

I know I should stop now. I am at a crossroads. I have convinced myself that he is going to dump me tonight. I have prepared myself for the end. I can see the finish line. I can actually feel how great it would be to be a part of Harris. To be a couple. But I am not letting it happen. I am choosing to obliterate what is not 100 percent perfect. I hate myself even before I smash the fragile union that is Harris and Maria to smithereens. But I am doing it anyway. I look at Harris, a pink mollusk without his shell.

"You always stand too close to people," I tell him, gulping for air. "You laugh too loud and suck up to people because of their social standing."

"No, I don't," he says.

"Oh yeah, then why did we traipse up to Maine? We being me, and your little sidecar, the Irish wonder," I add.

"I like the people in Maine. They're good at the sports I like to do. I think parties are fun. And Fin has been a very good friend to me," he answers in measured tones.

"Well, why aren't you sad about the baby?" I ask. I am breathing hard. My heart physically hurts, sharp shooting pain. I want to cry, but no tears come.

For this he has no retort. "You're a nice girl," he says. "Why don't you go home and get some rest?"

"I want to know why you are doing this," I say, feeling completely responsible and wishing I could have a do-over.

"I am tired of you judging me, Maria," he responds.

Now I really do hate him. How dare he act all sane and calm? Can't he see I am in pain? Don't we all judge each other all the time? And then, to add insult to injury, he easily hails a cab. He ushers me in, hands me a twenty, and closes the door between us.

"I just got dumped," I announce to the cab driver.

"It happens," he says and shrugs.

JUNE 28 I am pacing up and down in my two-room apartment. If I stop moving my internal elevator starts careening, and I can't stop it. Maybe Harris is right and he is not a social climber. Maybe he just spends a good part of his life scoring tickets to parties and invitations to people's country homes because it is fun. Or maybe he runs marathons and scores invitations incessantly for the same reason I keep moving tonight, because if I stop the pain will just be too great.

I am flabbergasted by my own eruption. Why did I need to destroy the last good thing left in my life? I need to go on one of those daytime talk shows, and get a goddamn diagnosis. Is it fear of failure? Or worse, fear of success? I get there. I am perfectly positioned, and I bolt. Maybe I could pitch my story as a prime-time sitcom: *Disaster Girl* starring Maria O'Mara. Watch her wacky fuck-ups. Every opportunity presented to her on a silver platter, dashed. Lifetimes of the almost rich and not so famous. I don't quite have the hook, but I've got the whole night to work it out. I wonder how long before I tire myself out, and I can finally sleep. Not yet. I need to keep moving even if I don't get anywhere, a dangerous metaphor often encountered by those on the brink.

"Harris, I am sorry," I say into the telephone. I have waited until 5 A.M.; that's restrained, isn't it?

"Maria, go to sleep," he says into the phone, and then a *click*. He is finished. Not okay I know you're sorry. No kissy kissy making up. A line has been drawn, and I am the one with the fucking crayon. The smoking crayon. Why couldn't I have just kept my mouth shut? I need duct tape to date. Maria O'Mara—you know her, she's the chick with the tape across her mouth. But when she takes it off, watch out. What technique! That could work. A person can have a lot of good ideas if they stay up all night and just think about things. Why did I yell at Harris?

JULY 8 I look into the eyes of a homeless guy in the subway station at Columbus Circle. He looks back. There is that moment of recognition. A compadre. Another one is going down. He can see it in my eyes. And I can see the depths in his. My elevator rides don't even begin to go there. But I am on my way. I climb the steep steps and get out on the northeast corner, the park side. It smells of horse shit. Maybe I should flag a horse and carriage, and go for a ride, maybe not. I inch my way over the cobblestones in my Italian heels on my way to work. Rejection as art, just another place I don't belong. Another failure on my long list. Wee, and we're off.

"Maria, I need a list of all of your clients and the progress of any deals in play," The Radical Theatre Agent snips as he dashes off to another, more important meeting to which all losers are clearly excluded. All losers, that means, now let's see . . .

"I wonder if they have already filled my slot?" I ask Jed in a too loud voice right out in the hall in front of God and everyone.

"Jeez, Maria," he says while simultaneously doing the universal *shh* sign. "You look . . ." He falters for the words.

"Want to go for a carriage ride through Central Park?" I ask.

He seems to be honestly considering it.

"It's just a job," Jed says as we ride through Central Park.

"I've never done this," I say, referring to our ride as I try to talk over my sage assistant. He is twenty-two, he's got his whole career ahead of him. "It's my life," I blurt out. "It's all I got."

"No, it's not," Mr. Connecticut-Country-Club, Deferred-Admission-to-Harvard-Business-School snaps back.

"Yes, it is, because when I don't have this job my phone will stop ringing and there are just not all that many openings for B-list players," I say in the voice of a cold clinician. I think of all of the names on my call sheet that I have called back at odd hours in the hopes of avoiding them. People I deemed aging losers. "Do you believe in karma?" I ask Jed.

"Maria, you have got to get a fucking grip," he says with no humor as we make our way past the carousel in a horse-drawn carriage in the middle of the workday.

JULY 11

Everyone in New York City has a shrink, and I have elicited a referral from each of them. Every scrap of paper in my possession has a number on it. It is 4 A.M. Another sleepless night. I am reviewing the mounds of little papers I have accumulated in the hopes that the spirits will direct me to the proper party. I would like to find the scrap of paper with the name of the shaman who "cleared" my office for four hundred bucks. You weren't supposed to clear it of me, you fucking idiot.

Not sleeping and eating frees up a lot of time. I should have tried this years ago. Plenty of time for pacing back and forth in seven hundred square feet, that is now a proven fact. If I stop I feel the void, and then the elevator starts. It is essential to keep moving.

The first shrink is just a few blocks north and west of me. I push the brownstone's buzzer. The door clicks, and I am in.

"Come on up," yells a voice. I make my way up steep wrought-iron stairs. It is one of those spiral jobs usually used to display houseplants. I finish my ascent and land in a dark little office. This guy's Upper West Side office reminds me of a movie set. A lot of faux charm. Monochromatic photographs of civil rights marches adorn the walls. A gray-haired fellow shrouded in a haze of pipe smoke coughs. He sits at a rolltop desk.

"Hello, he says and gives another cough. He looks at a Post-it stuck on his swivel chair. "Hello, Maria," he starts again as he roles his chair away from the desk and across from the modern designer chair—Eames, I think—in which I am meant to sit. He nods approvingly as I take my place. He's clearly into civil rights and modern design. I look around for a Ben Shahn drawing, but to no avail. We sit quietly for a few moments. Breathing and staring.

"Well," he finally says.

"Well, I am pretty upset," I say. "I feel as if I am losing control."

"Of what?" he says.

"Of everything," I say.

"Well." He coughs.

"Well, I had a miscarriage. I lost my job. I said mean things to my boyfriend, and now he is gone," I sort of blurt out.

"Do you have trouble with relationships?" the shrink questions.

"You could say that," I concede.

The little man nods and writes furiously on his yellow pad.

"Does that mean something?" I ask.

"Maybe," he says. "Are you depressed? Angry? Disorganized?" he questions enthusiastically.

My thoughts focus on the boxes from my office piling up in the foyer and living room of my apartment. "Well, I mean, I feel really bad—and my apartment is kinda messy." I trail off. This is not going well. I am feeling worse. The little man across from me keeps scribbling.

"Could be a personality disorder," he says.

"A what?" I ask.

"Could be a borderline personality," he says.

"What do you do for that?" I ask.

"I am really not sure," he says. "It's hard to treat. In fact I saw something on the Internet that said a lot of mental health professionals won't even try," he continues.

"Why not?" I ask.

"Burnout," he says.

"What?" I ask.

"The patients are just too hostile." He coughs. He turns to his computer and starts typing. "I'll print out the article for you."

I am exhausted. I have not slept all night. "Excuse me," I say.

"Yes?" he responds, intently focused on his computer screen.

"What exactly is your background?" I ask. I am in trouble. But this doesn't seem right. Is this the guy that the receptionist at work referred me to? I think his name was the one on the blue slip of paper.

"I have a Ph.D. in education," he says proudly.

This is a movie. This asshole doesn't know his ass from a hot rock. He read about this on the friggin' Internet?

"I am going now," I say.

"Of course—because you are incapable of facing your issues." He smiles. "Wait, I can print out the definition of borderline personality disorder."

And then I do lose it. The wall between my internal thoughts and my voice caves. "You, my little elf-man, are a fucking idiot,"

I screech. "How can you diagnose someone after three sentences? You read about this on the fucking *Internet?*"

"Borderlines are always so hostile." He nods knowingly. He is standing up now. "I know your type," he continues.

"You are crazy," I say as I try to descend the steep spiral stairs.

"That's the pot calling the kettle black," he laughs.

"I am calling the cops," he yells. "I am dialing right now."

"You're fucking insane," I yell from the bottom of the stairs.

"Hey, I was there in '61, bitch—I can handle the likes of you," he yells back.

I open the door back out onto the street. My head is throbbing. What was that? I am running through the Upper West Side. It is hot and muggy. I am exhausted. What the fuck is going on?

JULY 15 "Maria? Can you hold for The Radical Theatre Agent?" a voice says.

I am too busy pacing to answer the phone. I now know empirically that heat rises. It is 120 degrees in my little hot box on the eleventh floor.

"Ah, Maria," The Radical Theatre Agent begins, "we are still paying you. You must come to the office. And I must have that list of clients and deals," he demands. "Okay, roll the next call," he tells his assistant.

"Okay, but we have to hang up first," she tries to explain.

"Learn how to roll a call, would you?" he screams. "There is a rhythm!" And then a dial tone.

My limbs are so loose I can easily do the splits. I wonder if it is from the moist heat or if it has to do with my pregnancy. My bones knit their way wide to make room for Baby Harris. I walk more quickly across the important Oriental rug that is the property of my landlady. I wonder if I am unglued because of hormones. What are hormones anyway?

"Ah, Maria, this is Mark. I am the therapist you called. I can see you tomorrow morning at seven A.M. My address is 160 East Twelfth Street. So please call to confirm. *Click.*" More words wafting in the hot air draining the little oxygen I have left.

"I'll call you when it cools down," I say to the answering machine as I march past. I am on patrol in my living room. Hup two three, hup two three . . .

JULY 16 It is 3 A.M. I am still pacing, and not a bit tired. The more I try to tire myself out the more agitated I become. I am going over every detail of my relationship with Harris. The first mistake was tracking him in the snow. If he had wanted me he could have found me in the crowded room. Isn't that how fate works? I tried to impose my will on fate and she spit in my face. And then there was the fact that I wasn't more supportive. Harris paid so much attention to "the group," and I didn't pay any, and now I am fired. Expelled from the group. In a capitalistic society that means NO MONEY. Harris was just looking out for our economic interest. It was all my fault. If only I could explain to him that I understand. But I am too mean. He doesn't want to speak to me. I may have a personality disorder, but I wouldn't let the guy print out the definition so I can't be sure. Another mistake. I must go online and find out about this disorder—that is, as soon as I can stop pacing and concentrate.

I am standing in a dilapidated building in the East Village. It's the kind of building that housed private eyes in the 1940s, or at least in '40s movies. Beveled glass on the doors hides each office from view. The door I am meant to enter is locked. Faint ambient street noise wafts up the floors. It is eerily quiet for the city. I wait for another professional so I may relate my story. And then a huge African American man wearing high-top Nikes and a gray sweatsuit is upon me. Where did he come from? Is this how it will end? Brutally attacked and murdered on the eighth floor of a stiflingly hot building? Who gets murdered at 7 A.M.? Early risers.

"You Maria?" he demands.

"Yes," I say.

He unlocks the door of an office in which I am sure we will find Sam Spade. No such luck. Just a battered couch, an old leather chair, and a noise machine. He plugs in the noise machine and places it in the "outer office," a cramped space with one ladder-back chair. I remain standing.

"Now you can't hear no one, and they can't hear you," he explains. Who referred me to this guy?

I take my place on the couch as he fills up the entire leather chair. He seems to have grown even larger in the few moments that comprise our relationship. We engage in the requisite staring contest. This time I will not take the bait. Let him do the talking. He tenaciously waits. He gets paid for the hour whether I talk or not. I remain firm.

And then finally: "What do you want?" he asks.

"What?" I question.

"Well, you called me," he explains.

I'm pleased that he has spoken first. I believe I have won this round. I think about his question.

"I guess I want a Do-Over," I reply. Succinct and to the point; I am pleased with my response. Let's see what he does with it. He looks at me wide-eyed.

"No Do-Overs," he retorts.

"Are you sure, because—"

"Quit wasting time," he commands.

We sit silently. My heart pounds in my ears. Now what? He squints in my direction. Is he in contemplative mode? He squints. And I pay?

"What do you want?" he asks again with just a hint of exasperation.

"Well, I'd like my baby, boyfriend, and job back," I explain, elaborating on the "Do-Over" theme.

He shakes his head no. Tsk, tsk. I have fucked up again. Wrong answer, Maria. Where is the trapdoor? He continues to shake his head in disapproval.

"Look," I say, wishing to get this show on the road, "I am frightened and alone."

"What are you scared of?" he asks.

Good question. I have no response.

"You aren't scared of me," he remarks.

How can I tell him that out in the hall I was hoping that he would be the one to put me out of my misery, one quick snap of my neck in his large hand, and then the void.

It is getting hotter in the cramped little office. A thin layer of perspiration dances through my silk slip-dress. What are we doing here?

And then he starts—once again for the fans at home: "What do you want?" he emphatically demands.

"Why do you keep asking me that?" I question, wondering what the name of this particular brand of therapy might be.

"Because if you don't know what you want then you'll get nothin', and I don't believe you could live with that, Miss Maria O'Mara," he answers firmly.

Awfully presumptuous, but effective. I scroll through the crenellations of my brain searching for an alternative response. It repeatedly spits out "Do-Over." I wait a respectful amount of time and then I respond.

"I guess I just want to get up off this couch and catch the B train," I finally say.

"It's your choice," the gigantic therapist responds with a sad sigh.

"Well, thanks for your help," I remark awkwardly as I write out the check.

"Later," he says as he snatches the check from my hand.

"Yeah, much later," I say aloud as I walk along East Twelfth Street with nowhere cool to go in a city that is just starting to broil.

My feet are bathed in sweat and blood as I make my way up Central Park West. How better to kill a couple of hours than walking home from the East Village? I am focusing on the pain. So much better in my feet than my soul.

Harris still refuses to speak to me, but I persist in calling. And he persists in hanging up. Does he just get to plant his seed, and then when it all goes south, bolt? The answer, a resounding yes. New York City's credo is greed. Get as much as you can and pay for nothing. Harris is on the make. He certainly has no time for an empty vessel that once housed his genes. He is running to the finish line. He will be a winner. Despite the harsh results I see his point. And then the friggin' elevator starts.

I am rushing to my death accompanied by blisters. And then with the elevator going and the heat seeping up through my burning feet I am grabbed from behind. Angry arms jolt me from my thoughts. I am whisked up against the Beresford on the corner of Eighty-first and CPW. What will he do with me? The strength connotes a man. It is all happening rather slowly. No time for fear. Just waiting to see.

"You cunt," wails my assailant in a British accent. Huh, I got a British mugger. The juxtaposition of the big black shrink from hours ago and this upper-crust killer is not lost on me. Amazing how much time there is to think when one is being attacked.

The back of my head hits the rusticated façade. Even the buildings are hot. The assailant pushes my shoulders back so they too will know the heat. I am so plugged with adrenaline these days these few added insults seem mild. I am actually enjoying the pulsating pain from my head to my toes. I am paying for my mistakes and it feels good.

"Will you even be in show business now? You worthless little . . ."

I look into the tired eyes of my attacker. "Barry," I whisper. "Aren't you under house arrest?"

"I snuck out."

"You can go to jail for that."

"Never mind," he says. "How could you fuck me like this?"

"I got fired," I say meekly.

"So go somewhere else," he screams, still seething. I guess he has some abandonment issues.

"I can't," I say.

"You are so fucked up," he clamors.

I don't have the energy or desire to tell him of the fruitless interviews. He breathes heavily, still pressing his fingernails into my shoulders. I squirm and he lets go.

I feel the back of my head. A big bump is definitely forming. Assaulted by the client. So what else is new?

"You look like shit," he says. "Why are you limping?"

"Blisters," I say hoarsely. "You better come up to my place," I say in my best Humphrey Bogart tones. "We've got to get you back to Malibu Prep before the narcs sing and they slam your ass in county jail."

"You really look awful, old girl," he says.

"Look, Barry, I am having a nervous breakdown. Okay?" I demand, annoyed.

"Who isn't?" he asks.

I wait with Barry downstairs for the car service. We stand hand in hand. He understands. My view of all this is very ugly. We are two very spoiled people. I know it. I am not sure he does. He is a great director. Perhaps it comes with the territory. I have no excuse.

"Crocodile Boy really does love my work, doesn't he?" he says with a half smile.

"Yes," I say even though it is killing me. In a few months Barry will forget I was ever his agent. The baton has been passed. As long as Barry continues to thrive, Crocodile Boy will hang on, but if the career falters, look out. I probably was not made for this line of work.

Sick old Barry jams his tongue down my throat for our parting smooch. And I let him. A whore till the end. Well, actually more like a Polish whore—they fuck me and I pay. I must do something about that. I add it to the long list of repairs I am meant to do once I get all of my strewn parts back in some semblance of the self I have known for all of my forty odd years.

JULY 26 What does one wear to the last day of work? Definitely something with a cinched waste. All of those other size twos better watch out. Starving Agent Girl . . . Ladies and gentlemen, Maria O'Mara, come up on stage and take a bow. I am learning to live with the filmy view of one who never eats or sleeps. I am beyond anger. I am over the edge in a barrel and it is dark in here. The rest of Manhattan has my permission to race on by. Go get 'em, guys. I have no context. Locale is a mere technicality. I can easily get lost in my own apartment, in my own thoughts. There is one constant: the rapidly descending elevator. Plunging to new depths daily. No relief, no tears, and soon no money. I am getting to know the no's.

I pick a dress that I think used to be a long shirt, tie one of the ropy curtain tiebacks from the bedroom curtains around my waste, and I am ready. So ready. Calvin fucking Klein, eat your heart out. I am a genius. Pornographic Starving Agent Girl in a see-through shirt cinched by a curtain rope. Bravo, *moi*. And then

I pack an overnight bag. Flimsy lingerie, party dress, jeans, a sweater, and three pair of high heels. It is good to have choices. I am mounting a plan.

"What do you have on?" Jed asks as we take down my framed poster of Audrey Hepburn looking in the window of Tiffany's from my office wall.

"You just noticed?" I say. "It's deconstructivist. Isn't it fabulous?" I smile.

Jed winces. My smile is the edgy smile of one of those people on the street who talks to themselves. Everyone knows, but I keep singing. Da da da.

"There's no business like show business," I sing.

I have been taking boxes home all week so the office is pretty emptied out. Now for the finishing touches. Any hint that Maria O'Mara was ever here will be erased.

"Do you have a sweater?" Jed says, still worrying about my fashion statement.

"Who cares?" I smile. "We're not in Connecticut anymore, Toto," I say as I pat his arm. Da da da, the jolly firee.

Why is it that endings are always so anticlimactic?

"Bye," I say as I hand my key card to the overstuffed HR type.

"Bye," she says. "We'll miss you," she adds to show good sportsmanlike conduct.

"But you never liked me," I say.

"I know," she says and shrugs.

And that, ladies and gentlemen, is the end. Everyone else is secreted away in some "meeting." Its specified purpose: let's hide until she is gone. Ta-da. Another career dashed.

Jed stands at the building's West Fifty-third Street entrance with my meager boxes and now-cracked poster. Holly Golightly and seven years of bad luck all in one careless moment. I drive my car up to the curb, and we hurriedly load.

"We *are* in the loading zone," I scream to no one in particular.

Jed winces again. I don't think he has ever seen this before. I am sure I have not acted it before.

"Good-bye," I say as I throw my arms around his neck.

"Hey, Maria, I'll still call and stuff. Don't worry," he says. It is he who is worried. I imagine his visions of me rolling into Westport as the new Homeless Person. Out in front of Brooks Brothers trying to talk to him about the good old days.

"Don't you worry," I say. "I am on the mend."

"Okay," he says. And then I get in the car. And he walks back into my old life without me.

I am inching along the Long Island Expressway. It is too hot. All of the ants are seeking escape. I am resolute. I will put a big Band-Aid on all of this. My cell phone starts blaring.

"Hello," I scream into it over a certain amount of static.

"Hey," says Jed barely loud enough to be heard.

"Couldn't stand being without me, eh?" I scream.

"They want the phone back," he screams. Of course they do. My umbilical cord to the stars.

"Tell them I am on my way out of town," I scream.

"What?" he screams.

"Monday," I scream. "I'll get it to them Monday."

And then the phone goes dead. I hope ten movie stars call me over the weekend. I'll direct all of their calls to competitors.

Maybe they've already turned the friggin' thing off. I toss the phone out the car window. Too bad. All of those potential stars obliterated on the rough hard pavement of the L.I.E.

I am enjoying the shade. My feet rest upon a pillow of mud. The coolness is a relief after my four-hour car ride. I am on patrol. Every few moments I close my eyes and almost doze. And then I am shaken back to a conscious state. Waiting and watching from my lair. Only a lone unknown car. Then two young girls leading their horses back to a nearby stable. I don't mind. I am in no hurry. I am focused and ready. And then just when my legs are beginning to rebel against their crouched position I hear it—the incessant hacking of the old jeep. I peer out around the nearest bush and my heart stops. Harris is seated in the jeep. He is wearing a navy blazer, blue shirt, and white ducks. Where did he get those pants? He depresses the gas and ever so carefully lets out the old clutch. Sputter, sputter, splat, the car dies. My feet scrape up against the worn pavement as I scurry to my own car secreted around the corner. It is a pleasant sensation. For the first time since the miscarriage I am experiencing hope. I will fix this. I must.

As soon as Harris heads into the intersection I slowly begin to follow. It is tricky staying far enough behind to not be noticed, but close enough to follow. We are on Route 27 heading to Easthampton. Although I have no immediate plan I applaud myself for being totally in the moment. I drive with a skill heretofore unknown. I am keenly aware of my senses. So this is how it feels to be on the verge of success.

Harris heads into one of the toniest Easthampton hoods. Of

course. He heads up a long gravel road. There are gates. Big Gates. Shit. Another car pulls up behind him. The gates open. And then just as they close, another car turns onto the gravel road. It appears to be a steady stream. A party. La-dee-dah. I head into town to prepare *ma toilette*.

I pull into the public parking lot behind Main Street, more specifically behind the local Polo store. I pull my party dress from my overnight bag and head into the public rest room. It is a little tough getting my feet washed in the sink while standing, but the mud has definitely got to go. What the hell—I haul my ass up on the edge of the sink and stick my feet right in. I have to wait for the automatic faucet, which seems to have a mind of its own, but despite this minor inconvenience things are going well. That is, until some Little Leaguer and her mother show up. Refugees from the adjacent baseball diamond.

"Oh, my God," the proper Easthampton mother snarls. I pretend I don't hear her.

"Mommy, what is that lady doing?" the Little Leaguer asks. I smile at the kid. She smiles back.

"Just go to the bathroom," the mother snaps.

"Jeez," says the kid.

Jeez indeed. I've got a party, lady, relax.

My skintight red dress is a little less than skintight. When you lose weight do you lose skin? My hair is brushed. Plenty of lip gloss. Proper black mules, little black handbag. I am party ready. I park around the corner from The Gates, and head up the gravel road on foot. Another challenge, gravel and little black mules.

"I am up to the challenge," I say aloud, just in case I forget as I wobble up the road. And then the gods descend. A catering van is heading up the road.

"Need a ride?" the college kid who is masquerading as a caterer asks.

"Great," I say as I make the sign of the cross (blessing myself) and climb into the van.

The house is an important one, architecturally, that is. It is modern and asymmetrical. The smell of money wafts. I start to follow the college boy caterer into the kitchen.

"Ma'am, I think you'll want to go in the front door," he instructs.

Ma'am? I have got to do something about that. I take a deep breath and aim in the direction of my proper entrance. I enter easily and saunter over to the bar, undetected.

It is a group of about twenty, and I surmise a sit-down. Oh, well, perhaps I'll just stay for cocktails. The thug quotient is high. It feels very show business, but I don't see anyone I know, including Harris.

"A margarita, please," I say to the bartender. He nods. And then as I turn, drink in hand, I see Harris across the room. And he sees me. His face falls. He looks ill. I take a hefty swig, and prepare to stand my ground. It's a party. Plenty of room in this huge loft of a house even for the uninvited. No reason to freak or anything. Harris walks slowly but determinedly in my direction. I take another swig.

And then I hear, "I thought she got fired," and I turn. There in his signature black T-shirt and navy blazer is fucking Max Rubin.

"Only from the Agency, Max, not from life," I retaliate.

Finally Harris has found a group I can work and I am history. I don't really like this position. Now I am not descending rapidly. Now I am at the bottom of a big fucking hole, and I am clueless as to how to get out. Perhaps this wasn't such a good idea.

"Who is she?" inquires a large thug dressed in a Hawaiian shirt and khakis. Why doesn't anyone speak to me directly? How rude.

"I am Maria," I say directly. And then I notice the female guests who have headed over in the direction of drama. They all look about twelve years old—long legs, blonde hair, and flat exposed stomachs. "What did you do—empty out the Junior Miss Pageant?" I ask.

"I don't like this broad," The Hawaiian Shirt says. "Hey, look, lady, they are all legal," he continues just to cover his ass.

"What are you doing now, Maria?" Max asks with a sneer, in an attempt to expose and obliterate me.

"I am up for a job running a network," I say.

"Who the fuck would be stupid enough to hire you for that job?" Max snaps back.

Oh, what fun. I take the last swig of my margarita.

"Well, they can't do any worse than they are doing now," I say with all of the bravado I can muster.

"Jesus, is it ABC?" Max asks with a twinge of awe. "I didn't know she knew Eisner," he continues to no one in particular. "How do you know Michael Eisner?"

Uh-oh, does eagle-eye Max smell a rat? Harris is waiting in the wings to see how things turn out. Perplexed about his next move.

"You are so literal," I say to Max.

"What the fuck does that mean?" Max snarls.

"Is she, like, some old movie star or something?" one of the twelve-year-olds asks.

I suppose I could be a movie star. Thanks, honey. I like that one.

"It's just cable, isn't it?" Max asks. He is such a mastermind.

"Max, why do you always wear black T-shirts with navy blazers? It looks terrible," I say just to keep the party moving.

"Maria, go fuck yourself," says Max in an offhanded manner.

"Now you'll never sell those shit TV movies, Max." I smile.

"There are a lot of cable stations, baby," he says and smiles back.

"Who invited her?" The Hawaiian Shirt asks, back to the matter at hand.

"If you're worried about place settings, I won't be staying for dinner," I say. "Just dropped by for a cocktail," I quip.

"I'll take care of this," says Harris in officious tones. He sees his moment and he is seizing it. The little social grifter will take care of the interloper and, voila, he will have arrived in thug society.

"I can see myself out," I reply, remembering my very best ballet school posture.

"Is she leaving?" one of the twelve-year-olds inquires.

So sorry, doll, got to dash. I turn and head for the door, noticing a lot of gold records on the wall. I guess Mr. Hawaiian Shirt is in the record business. Harris accompanies me. Once we are outside he discards the mellifluous tones.

"Maria, leave me alone," he shrieks. "Get out of my life. And stop following me, or I will fucking have you arrested, and I am not kidding," he continues, shaking with rage. This was not quite the reunion I imagined. No kiss? No making up? How could such a simple plan go so wrong?

I contemplate the long walk down the gravel path, and feel defeated as Harris heads back inside. For the first time I notice a massive sculpture on the lawn. It is a complex entwined body of wire and steel.

"I know," I say to the sculpture, feeling impotent and desperately wishing I could cry.

Someone opens the front door. Shit. They probably have put out an APB. I start my uneven walk on the sharp little rocks back to life on the other side of The Gates.

"Hey, wait up," calls an unfamiliar voice. A handsome man I believe is a painter joins me on the path.

"That was brilliant." He is smiling.

"Which part?" I inquire.

"Well, I particularly liked the part where you told the short producer where to go," he answers.

"Yeah, I am good at that," I say. I turn and keep walking. Inch by inch on the uneven surface in my little heels.

"May I call you a cab?" the handsome painter continues.

"No, thanks," I say, still trying for a graceful exit.

He continues to try to accompany me. "I'd like to help," he tries again.

"Beyond help," I brusquely reply, all of the while praying I will not fall face first into the sea of gravel.

"You're really hurting," the handsome painter notes.

"Yeah," I say, still attempting my exit.

"I have a terrific shrink," he continues.

"You and everybody in friggin' New York," I say.

"Really. This guy is an M.D. He'll give you drugs," he adds.

"No, thanks," I say.

"Well, here is his card anyway," he says.

"Okay," I say, still walking away.

"You'll be fine," he says. "You're really something," he continues as he walks back to the house.

"Glad to be of some amusement," I whisper, hoping that this road is not as long as I remember.

I am driving west on Route 27, back toward the city. There must be some payoff for being beyond humiliation, but at the moment I can't see it. The air is moist, and although I can't see a friggin' thing it feels verdant. And there is that smell. The promising summer one. I may be able to smell it, but I am definitely not going to be able to live it. My name must be on a list. Harris's image, his expression filled with disgust, keeps coming to mind. I wonder if he can get a temporary restraining order after only one party crash. Shit. I am in trouble. I know it. And I don't know if I can stop it. Who knew you can actually watch yourself go mad? Oh, well. At least I am finally a size two. I always wondered what that would be like. I may have given up a little too much to find out.

My arms and legs are suddenly heavy with fatigue. I think I may have finally worn myself out. I make a right turn onto Bridgehampton Turnpike and head to a beach I know. I am going to park the car and sleep. Finally sleep. Maybe it will all look better in the morning. Yeah, right.

JULY 27 When I awaken I am even more tired than I was when I curled up in the back seat of my car. But I get to watch the dawn. It is glorious, and I know it. I think that is a good sign. I get out of the car, and stand on the edge of Noyack Bay waiting for the sun. The gray-blue light is calming. I walk into the water. The cold feels good. Now my feet are awake, but the rest of me is still tired. I am still wearing my red dress, but so what? I wade out a little farther and dive in. Maybe the cold water will be curative. I do a gentle crawl parallel to the shore. And then I float on my back and gaze at the pale pink clouds in the violet sky.

"Well, I am totally fucked," I say to the clouds and the sky. They smile back. Nature could give a shit whether I am a duck or a fish or a former theatrical agent floating in the bay. The sun's still going to shine, and those assholes from that party last night are still going to spend money and swagger, and there is not a thing I can do about either.

No towel, oh, well. I shake myself off and get back in the car. I can see that not caring is going to free up a lot of time.

"I am heading out," I announce to the folks at home. After all, I am here for their viewing pleasure. Why else would all of this be happening? I wish the guy with the easy smile and the camera crew would show up soon, though, because I don't know if I have the stamina for too much more.

I am back on Route 27. I am tired but resolute; one foot in front of the other. And then the friggin' elevator starts again. I am plummeting. I try to focus on the road but am confronted by something plastic and wavering.

I carefully pull the car onto a dirt shoulder in front of a vegetable stand. Too early for them, but not for this. I can't stop it. I am panicked. I crawl out of the car and sit in the dirt wishing it would go away. How much plunging can one person take? The backs of my hands are drenched in sweat. So unseemly. I dust off, get back in the car, and drive to a gas station.

I stand expectantly in a sun-drenched telephone booth, waiting and listening.

"Hello," says the voice at the other end of the line after thirty-six rings.

"Hello," I say back. "I was referred to you by your patient. The one whose work is in the Modern. He may be in the Met too, but I am not sure," I begin. It is always good to lead with one's credentials.

"Yes?" the voice asks.

"I'd like to see you," I say.

"I see," says the voice. And then nothing. What? He can't

locate me? I am an acquaintance of the painter, and I am losing my mind. Ah.

"I am losing my mind," I add, hoping to get this show on the road.

"How so?" questions the shrink.

"It feels as though I am making continuous rapid descents in a rickety elevator," I explain. Now I am pissed. Just fucking cure me, big shot. "I need to come today."

"It's Saturday," the voice answers.

Saturday, Thursday, what's the difference? Now I do a long pause.

"Alright," he finally says. "Come at two o'clock."

"Where are you?" I ask.

"Central Park West and Ninetieth Street," he says. "Saturday appointments are highly unusual," he adds.

"I didn't go to agent school for nothin'," I reply.

"I beg your pardon?" he says.

"Nothing," I say. And then I inch my way back to the car, and the hope that I can keep moving forward.

I am seated on the faux marble floor outside the newest shrink's office. It is cool. I have carried my overnight bag from the car up to the building. Of course I walked. No cabs for me. I am quite early. A ringside seat at my own demise. I wait and doze. And then, finally, a modern-day Abe Lincoln, right here in New York City. Hey, buddy, is that face the result of plastic surgery? I'll have the kind and craggy face, please. Oh, the Abe Lincoln Special, *no problema*. Or is it just the genetic lottery? Hey, my shrink is a direct descendant of friggin' Abe Lincoln. May I just call you Abe?

Is it still Saturday? I've been camped out here so long I've lost track.

"Maria?" old Abe inquires.

"The one and only," I reply.

"Planning on staying a while?" He smiles as he takes in my overnight bag. Ah, a player.

"Depends." I smile as I move away from the locked door and he lets us both in. Okay, buddy, do your magic. It is a one-bedroom apartment on Central Park West gone shrink, austere fifties décor. Still no Ben Shahn drawing, but definitely moving in that direction. Any member of the New York intelligentsia would be entirely comfortable spilling his guts in a joint like this. Yes sirree.

We settle in. He in his chair. Eames? No doubt. And me on the leather couch. Would that be charcoal? Such a tasteful color.

"What's that smell?" inquires Abe.

I take a pointed whiff. "Oh, it's the sea," I answer back.

"I beg your pardon?" he says.

"I went swimming this morning," I explain.

He shrugs, pulls out a yellow pad, and we are off. We talk dead babies and social ambition and perilous elevator rides. After a few beats this guy seems to speak Maria. He's skilled, interested, but not surprised.

"I think you should come back tomorrow," he says as the hour comes to a close.

"Sunday?" I ask.

"Well, you know what day it is," he says and laughs.

"But Sunday?" I ask again.

"You didn't go to agent school for nothin'," he answers back. This guy is good.

I drop my overnight bag back at my apartment, take a shower, and I am ready. So ready, but for what? The rest of Saturday to kill and half of Sunday before I can go back to the safety of the shrink, and the microscopic inspection of my meaningless life. Where does one go waterskiing in New York City? It is summer. What about a weenie roast? Why pace at home when there is an entire maze of a city? Hot, relentless cement. Oppressive moist air, and steam. We got it all in the Big Apple. I head into the park. I have never seen so much happiness. Rollerbladers, sunbathers, bike riders, and babies. Dogs, couples, tourists, and babies. I hover outside my diminished self. I am an old shriveled piece of fruit. No fecundity. No babies. I rush east to get out of the park. Eager to beat the roller-coaster version of a plunge to my own depths, as if I have any. How can a person who has conducted such a superficial life know such depths? Something to discuss with the shrink. More pressure, topics for the shrink. Everything comes with responsibility. Carnegie Hill is a ghost town. I walk to the corner of Eighty-ninth and Park, and look both ways. They've all gone fishin'; every last Chanel-clad one of them. I wonder if they bus them out. Come on, you rich people, march. We ain't got all day. And so I scoot back to Madison. Imagine the markdowns, a regular field day. This town is my oyster. Never mind that I had to exterminate the competition. Well, okay, with a little help from the season. I imagine myself with a bazooka. Okay, you fucking Lotte Berk bimbos toned to perfection, you're toast. These size twos are mine, all mine.

And then in the distance, heading uptown straight toward me, is Wyatt James. I lick my lips in preparation. A friend. Someone to talk to. I do have a life. She looks great, all svelte and tanned. What's that color she is wearing? Is it periwinkle? Love the shift. Couture? And then she is upon me.

"Wyatt," I sort of shriek.

Her face falls into a most unattractive grimace. She's definitely not using Botox. "I am on the phone," she says as she moves rapidly away.

My heart sinks, but still no tears. What? You don't like blood-soaked, semistarved, out-of-work party favors? Did I forget to send a thank-you note for the miscarriage flowers? What?

JULY 28 "You look better," the shrink remarks at the onset of meeting number two.

"I feel worse," I reply. It occurs to me that the shrink thinks I always go swimming in my slinky red dress. No way, baby; I do designer. "I used to be charming."

"Good to know," the shrink says with a smile. "Listen, Maria, you have got to start pretending that you're okay."

"You mean like I have a job and a boyfriend?"

He shakes his head no. "As if you are not experiencing extreme difficulty," he says. Extreme difficulty? What the fuck does that mean?

"How bad is this?" I ask.

"On a scale of one to ten?"

"Okay," I say.

"Seven-and-a-half," he says. I like the half. "And I would like to start you on medication."

"Nope," I quickly reply.

"Why are you so resistant?" he asks.

"Look, my father was an anesthesiologist," I start. "You guys change your mind too often."

"I assure you that the medication will help you—"

"No drugs," I insist. "And I don't want to waste the hour discussing it." He nods.

"Do you have any plans?" he inquires, dutifully changing the subject.

Now, what the fuck is he talking about? Plans? I pace, I don't eat or sleep. I suppose that is a regimen of sorts.

"Maybe the law," I say.

We are now into ancient dialogue. College admissions crap. I seem to recall they always liked the law answer.

The shrink belts out a hearty laugh, his first in our burgeoning relationship. "Of course—you want to know the rules," he says, wiping at his eyes. Tears of joy, no doubt.

"The rules would be helpful," I say.

The shrink stares at me with his big old Abe Lincoln countenance. One of his eyes is definitely a lot bigger than the other. "I think you should write all of this down," he suggests.

"Document my insanity?" I question.

"It may help you to gain some clarity," he says.

"I think clarity is exactly what I am trying to avoid," I say.

"And I want you to set up some job interviews," the shrink continues.

Do they have Taco Bell in New York? I can't seem to remember. Maybe I can be a dog walker, then I could keep moving.

"Okay," I say with nothing in mind. What happened to the part where I whine, and old Abe Lincoln over there just shakes his head? I had to get a proactive shrink. What is up with that?

JULY 29 I am in Rizzoli on West Fifty-seventh Street trying to choose a diary. Excuse me, my psychiatrist suggested I write all of this down—do you prefer the red suede or leather bound? Which do you think is the real me? The short bald Italian standing next to me moves away. He senses I am nuts and in need of discussion. Too bad, I am fun, you pudgy little cigar-odored pug, you. I think the red suede, but then there is that plaid. How can one be sure?

I am marching uptown, armed with my red suede diary. Clarity is now an option, at least according to the shrink. Talk, talk, talk, write, write, write, and poof—the cure. But first I must set up some job interviews. He has got to be fucking kidding. Dude, I am so over. Didn't you get the memo? Dialing for jobs: Hello, yes, I am experiencing extreme difficulty and cannot get along with others. I am sure I am perfect for your company. Shall we meet?

JULY 31 I am in my apartment poised to dial. All dressed up, but no one to call. I try Harris out in Water Mill. He's very well connected, you know.

"Hello," he says after four long rings.

"Hello," I begin before the resounding dial tone. He's getting quicker; I will give him that. Too bad hanging up on old girlfriends is not an Olympic event. Then he could be well connected and a gold medal winner. Something to aspire to.

I open up one of the cardboard boxes from my office. All neatly packed up by Jed. Perhaps there is a name in one of the files, someone besides the shrink who didn't get the memo. I will pick seven random names from my old files and dial. What's the worst that can happen? Oh, that already happened. I am free. Now, whom will I pick?

"Hi, it's Maria," I start. Why not jump right in? Networking from thirty thousand feet. "O'Mara—from the Agency. Well, actually I've left. Uh-huh, I am not there anymore. Well, I'd love to come in and talk."

I am thwarted. He is shooting a movie, going on vacation, and probably moving to Paris. Do you think he just doesn't want to meet? I've heard paranoia is a side effect of going nuts, but come on! Okay, now I am mad. I am dialing for a friggin' meeting, not a job, just a meeting. I roll the Rolodex dice—*Baby needs a new pair of shoes!* I scream.

"Yes, Maria O'Mara. I'll hold," I say. Yeah, I'll hold till hell freezes over, you jerk. Just give me a meeting.

Twenty-four calls later I have scored two meetings. Not bad. Now what will I wear? Even though the words and the moment rarely coincide these days it is essential to look the part. I will dress my way out of this. That ought to work.

AUGUST 16 I trudge in to the shrink's. Now what to talk about? Why do I feel as if I have to please? I am fucking paying him. Now I am mad. Misdirected anger? A topic, thank God. Bring on the high-priced, Upper West Side psychiatrist. I am ready to wow!

"I don't want to do these meetings," I tell old Abe.

"Got to," he says. His lids are heavy. Sleepless night? Okay, okay, I know you have problems of your own. Let's change chairs. You pay and I'll listen.

"But I am fucking crazy," I say. "I'll blow it."

"Have you started writing down your thoughts?" he asks in the same bored tone.

"Not exactly, but I bought a diary," I say. I think about telling him it is red suede, but decide that is just too girl, even for me.

"Maria, I will be taking my annual vacation," he begins carefully.

It is close to the end of the hour and now he fucking throws this in? I refuse to display a reaction. I've lost more than you, buddy, much more.

"I am going to give you my number out on the island. We can retain our meeting times and do them telephonically," he explains in the same careful tones.

"Do I get a discount for that?" I ask.

He demonstrates no affect. And then in the final few moments I am frantic.

"I can't go to any meeting. My mind is broken," I say, but the shrink is having none of it. He will go off on his holiday, and I am meant to act as if. That is one big fucking IF.

I am walking in midtown. I am professionally clad: black Armani pants suit. It is hot. The city persists at a slightly slower pace. I am meeting an agent from a talent agency nestled somewhere below Fiftieth Street. Perhaps I can talk him into giving me a job. I try to think, but no thoughts come. I believe I am in the process of losing my mind. Why won't the shrink comment on this ultimate issue? Why did he insist I have this meeting?

"I can't go to any meeting. My mind is broken," I informed him at 8:45 this morning. "I don't even know the guy's name," I insisted.

"What guy?" he asked in a calm, thorough voice. He looked at me as if I were behaving oddly. I looked down to make sure I remembered to button my shirt. At this point even that is a question.

"Maria, you have got to fight this thing," the psychiatrist continually insists. What thing? I'm trying to get a name for what I have. I keep thinking if it had a name, then I could wrap my brain around it and squelch it. "I am not into names," the psychiatrist always informs. He obviously does not subscribe to my theory of naming it and squelching it, or he does and he really doesn't want to cure me. At least not so quickly that he can't add a couple of rooms onto his house out on Shelter Island.

Now I am in a coffee shop around the corner from the New York Yacht Club, waiting. I have no idea what I will say to a guy whose main claim to fame is booking a magician onto Letterman. He arrives. I still do not know his name, but I recognize him. Pencil thin, a suit that is too shiny, a mustache composed of perspiration and desire.

"Good to meet ya," he says as he sidles in without needing to pull out his chair.

He is the narrowest person I have ever seen, and he is weighted down by a gold medallion—an anchor he is attempting to pass off as jewelry.

"That's some necklace," I say, staring across the rickety table.

"A family heirloom," he responds as he reaches down to place a book of matches under an unstable table leg. One wrong turn and your life can be way off track.

"So what happened?" he asks. My brain is on strike. I stare at my roast beef sandwich. I want to put the sandwich into my mouth, but I am afraid to. On the other hand if I gag at least I won't have to answer.

"So?" he persists. He knows I lost my job. He wants reasons.

I rewind the recent past. I grab for an answer. Finally—"I am not good at men," I hear myself reply.

"Who is?" he says as he slathers mustard onto the moist rye

bread slapping at his pastrami. Eating in show business is supposed to be much more glamorous.

"Got any clients ya can bring over?" he hungrily demands. "It's all about bookings. If you got da bodies, I can get 'em da jobs."

I pull a tattered buck slip from my fine leather bag. My eyes dance down the list—prima donnas, habitués of '21' and Michael's, none of them big enough to forgo the trappings or save my job. "I'll have to get back to you on that," I say.

"Yeah, don't call us . . . I've heard it before," he says as he slams down only enough money for his sandwich.

"Okay," I say as he heads for the door. I am still seated in my plastic chair, starring at the ragged roast beef that I can't quite get to my mouth.

The heat burns through my clothes. The city bends around me. I see flashes of images, but they don't seem to fit. The sidewalk seems to be in the wrong place. The cars are all going backwards. I hear people uttering gibberish as I make my way across to Sixth Avenue. This is it. I have lost my mind. I fish around in my handbag for change. I hate that I had to give up my cellular phone. I am searching for a telephone booth. They are never there when you need one. I wonder if they have all just skipped off to another part of town.

I feel the heat of the sidewalk rise up through the soles of my shoes. My white shirt is wet and sticks to me like a paper towel. I start to punch the numbers of the only phone booth that has not escaped midtown.

"Hello, yes, I would like a room," I say into the receiver. "I really need a rest." I think my feet have developed third-degree burns. I wonder what communicable disease I am catching by talking on this pay phone.

The woman seated across from me is probably younger than I. She has no lines on her face, no straggling gray hairs. She definitely played field hockey at an earlier time. I think of her muscular legs racing up the field, pleated skirt flying, hockey stick firmly in hand. I bet she always knew she would be a psychiatrist.

"Well, why do you think you belong here?" she asks. I flash on an admissions office meeting at Yale, circa 1981. Same exact question. Same exact answer.

"I think it will be good for me and the institution," I posit. The field hockey–playing shrink looks worried.

"No, I mean what happened to you, to make you come here?" she tries again.

"Well, I had never really ridden the A train this far up before," I begin. Sometimes the narrative form is really helpful. I think I see her pushing a button on her desk. I wonder if the attendants will come in now.

"Are you presently under the supervision of a psychiatrist?" she demands.

"Yes," I say.

"And what is his name?"

"Arthur Schlossberg," I say.

"He runs this place," she says, almost not believing what she is hearing. "What does he think?" she asks.

"I don't know. He's gone to the country. Do you have the number?" I inquire. She just stares at me.

I pull out a pen and a pad from my purse and write down my psychiatrist's out-of-town number. She takes it. The young psychiatrist stands up. It is clear she is dismissing me from the locked ward. I look at her.

"Don't call us, we'll call you?" I query, parroting my thin agent friend from earlier in the day. She does not respond.

As I walk down the hallway this does not seem to be a place I would really enjoy staying. Yet I am still disappointed. I suppose it's a rejection thing. The black guard gives me a desultory glance.

"Didn't get in, huh?" he comments. I shrug and walk back out into the light. I am way uptown. I suppose it is time to go home.

The box boy at the market, who has been in and out of institutions for the greater part of his life, has diagnosed this as an agitated depression. Although I don't know the nomenclature it sounds plausible. When I get back to my apartment I remember I can't sit down. I can't stand still. And so I pace. Fortunately the park view makes it a slightly less than oppressive situation. But there is still no air-conditioning in the living room. It is hot. I keep moving and then when I can't stand the loneliness anymore I start dialing for dollars.

"Hi, it's Maria," I begin. "No, I didn't realize. It's 3 A.M.? I am really upset and—yeah, of course. We can talk later." I have called my old assistant and awakened him. Not good, but not as devastating as others of these calls I have made. Someone lower in the pecking order, well, a call like that can't be too bad. Unless of course he ascends to the position of studio head within the next twenty-four months and bad-mouths me all over town. I start pacing faster. Assessing the probable damage of this call to the would-be—whom am I kidding, almost-nearly-appointed—studio head, who is so pissed off that in a raging fit of narcissism I call him at 3 A.M. Oh, my God. I will never work in show business again. I pace even more frantically. Who can I call?

AUGUST 17 I am prostrate on the bedroom floor. One leg is extended underneath the bed. I am searching for a slip-on flat. It is still dark outside. I have an idea of someone who might talk to me at five A.M. I walk up Columbus Avenue with purpose. I know no one will bother me. I am too nuts and it shows. Yesterday I was walking in the park in suede loafers. It suddenly started to pour; I was umbrellaless. Even in my present state I was not about to ruin my shoes, so I took them off. When I reached my building I was drenched and shoeless. Freddie the doorman leered. I have reached that place where muggers won't bother and doormen know they have a shot—not good.

I head west on Eighty-fourth Street and there it is—my destination. I ring the bell. No answer. I lie on it for what seems an interminable amount of time. Finally, "Yes?" comes out of the speaker.

"Ah, this is Maria O'Mara, I would like to see a priest," I explain.

"Now?" the voice questions.

"Right now," I say with assurance.

There is a long pause, then another voice, a more authoritative gravelly one. "I'll be right down," this voice intones.

I wait on the sidewalk outside the iron gate. I pace as I wait. I don't think I have ever been here, but I know they have a Spanish mass.

An elderly Irish face peers out at me through the little window in the door. Perfect, I think. The guy could be a relative. Red-faced, deep-set light eyes, large nose—it is all familiar. He opens up the heavy door and leads me into a small room just to the left of the entrance.

Neither of us mentions the hour. I do not apologize. In my present state there is no room for that. He looks at me expectantly. I launch in.

"I've lost my mind. I need to speak with someone. I need help." I keep trying to think of something to say about God, as I am here and it seems such a mention would be a prerequisite to such a visit or at least establish some sort of entitlement. He still just stares. I wonder if he is asleep with his eyes open. In the light he does look like a horse to me. Finally I add, "Oh, I am a Catholic." Not a direct mention of God, but at least some credentials.

"I see," says the horse-faced priest. His teeth are too white. They must be false or maybe implants.

I keep staring back into the face of the expectant priest. I feel like he wants me to admit to a murder or perhaps an armed robbery, or a hit-and-run accident or a barroom brawl. I don't think he'd care, just something big to justify the hour. As much as I want to please him I am not about to lie to the clergy. I don't think he would be so interested in the fact that I got fired from a talent agency. I start to review the set of events that have led me here. It occurs to me that I believe I may have committed a murder, but I am not quite prepared to admit it. Not to him, and more importantly, not to myself. Now I have less to talk about.

"I can't catch my own thoughts, and I am frantic," I say, hoping that will illicit some reaction which will lead to a prayer, a blessing, and a polite invitation to depart.

"Are you under psychiatric supervision?" the tired priest asks. That question again.

"Yes, Father. I am," I uncomfortably admit.

"Are you takin' any medication, then?" he demands.

"What?" I say, not certain I have heard correctly.

"I am referrin' to antidepressants. You know, psychopharmacology is really quite advanced these days," he confidently continues.

Only in friggin' New York. I want to scream at him to act like a priest and give me a goddamn blessing, but I guess I am not quite that nuts, not yet anyway.

"No, Father, I am not taking any drugs," I answer.

"Well, you might look into it," he says as he stands up. I clearly am not going to invoke my priest/penitent privilege and confess to any murder, so he is going back to bed.

"What did you say your name was again?" he asks. He probably wants to put me on some priests' blacklist that will alert all Roman Catholic priests not to open their doors to me in the middle of the night or something. So, fine.

"Sally O'Casey," I answer back with the first name that pops into my head. Why give this drug-pushing Irishman with his sophisticated New York attitude any more information than he needs?

"Well, good luck to you, then, Sally," he says. He makes the sign of the cross vaguely in my direction and opens the heavy door with a nod, reminiscent of the nod one gives a dog being encouraged to go pee. I turn and walk out. Tah-tah, I think. Another unsatisfactory encounter.

When I return to my apartment I sit down and begin writing.

My full name is Maria Keril O'Mara. I am an out-of-work talent agent. My early training was that of a spy. I grew up in Southern California, specifically the San Fernando Valley. My father, John Francis O'Mara, was an anesthesiologist. My mother, Ines, is an interior decorator. My brother, Seamus, who is four years younger than I, was an outlaw—today he is a criminal prosecutor.

It was a tense household. My brother started dealing drugs at age nine. The first time my father caught him he confiscated my brother's scales. Seamus was devastated. My parents' fights (of which there were many) seemed to be locale based. In the car, they fought over freeways. Which ones to take, which ones they would have taken had their destination been different, and the third and most theoretical group: which ones presently under construction they might take if they chose to stay together. A possibility they both seemed to doubt vehemently. In the house they fought about décor. My mother was continually changing the interior. "Let's experiment," she would commence. And then she would paint the entrance hall bright red or move all of my father's things out of what had that morning been his study. My father's things would then be moved to another room or sometimes just stacked up in the hallway while my mother waited for her muse. This drove the old man crazy. He would come home from the hospital, tired and worried-looking, only to find that his things had been mislaid and that his wife and children were covered in paint. His face would turn all red and a litany of swear words would follow.

The most interesting aspect of their marital discord led to a game we called spying, whose full import it took me many years to decipher. It had to do with my father and a fair. The notion of a fair was particularly exciting. Some vague fantasy of green fields and balloons and other children with which to play always came to mind. My mother would say, "Whoever finds Dad has the sharpest eyes." Sometimes other kids from the neighborhood would join us, but principally it was just she and I (and later Seamus) who would pile into the car and head out into the yellow light in search of my father.

We never found my father or the fair. The most we ever discovered was my father's car parked in a motel parking lot on the outskirts of town. Because I always strove to please, it was usually I who found his car, but instead of pleasing her this revelation always seemed to make my mother mad. And so, having found no magical fair, we would head home and repaint the kitchen.

My parents remained married until the day my father keeled over in the operating room attempting to bag another patient. Seamus was sent off to boarding school. And I went to Yale, where I told everyone I was an orphan with some distant relatives in Paris. There is great freedom in invention. A self that is purely manufactured, that is simply the product of one's imagination, is capable of anything. At least until the implosion, or so I am learning.

It has been three hours since I left the priest. It is already hot in my apartment. I am standing in my tiny kitchen thinking of skiing. "Don't look at the trees. Look at the spaces between the trees," they keep shouting. The more they shout, the more I am sure that I am headed right for the trees. I think about the resulting decapitation, pleased that I won't have to pay off my Bergdorf bill, and then I am back, veering toward the trees, doing my damnedest not to hit them. After all, life is more or less a survival game. With a little luck—if you're still standing—you've got a shot. That's pretty much what I was thinking when Harris Schwartzman entered my life.

AUGUST 26 It is 4:45 A.M. I am not sleeping.

"Dr. Schlossberg?" I say into the telephone after only one and one-half rings.

"Yes," he answers back.

"It's Maria O'Mara," I say.

"I know," he says. Annoyance fills the airwaves.

"I tried to commit myself," I begin.

"I heard," he says, bored as can be with yesterday's news. Sorry, I didn't know it made the wire services.

"Dr. Schlossberg," I say again after a rather long beat.

"Yes, Maria," he says. More annoyance.

"I wrote everything down," I tell him.

"What did you learn?" he asks.

I think of the red suede diary completely filled with the tale of Harris and me. "Well," I say, stalling for time. And then finally: "I learned my middle name is regret."

"Keep writing," he says, and then a *click*. Nice, my shrink just hung up on me.

AUGUST 29 "Maria, this is your landlady. I've had an offer on the apartment that I think I am going to accept. I wanted to let you know as soon as possible because I know finding an apartment in New York City is not always easy. Call me." *Click* and then a dial tone.

I am awakened in my safety boat, the living room couch. I have burrowed into it. The bed is just too desolate. And even here I am not protected. Is there no free zone? I can't wait for my engraved invitation: "The City of New York respectfully requests that you kindly vacate . . ."

No job, no man, no progeny, and now no home. My limbs are heavy. I live inside of an unrelenting ache. I am famished, yet if I try to eat I am ill. I am documenting all of this in the little red book as if somehow it will make a difference. As if the words on the page will somehow be able to rearrange themselves into another life: "And then she got a fabulous job, and married the Count of . . ."

But I am still here. Just me and I am being evicted. I don't know what God thinks, but from my vantage point it doesn't seem to be turning itself around. It occurs to me that I am no less capable than any of those on the Manhattan sidewalks scurrying purposefully in every direction. Most people find a mate and pair off. Most people find a job and do it. I have been that person and I must insist that I will be again.

I untangle myself from the couch and head toward the kitchen. The smell of coffee fills the apartment. I amass the ingredients for corn muffins on the kitchen counter and go to work. My plan? To inch my way back one moment at a time. My slumber is constantly interrupted by my life's fractured remnants. I blame myself in large part for my failed relationship. I never said what I needed. I harbored resentment, and then when no one was looking shot poison darts in the direction of my not so significant other. It takes courage to say what you want and what you won't tolerate. And it takes compassion and humor to see through another's wavering defense system, and pull them toward you. We are all players in our own dreams, fraught with insecurity, desperate to be loved. I am intelligent enough to understand this, yet so far not mature enough to act as if I do.

As I mix the dough for my muffins in the heavy white bowl I vow to myself to get back in the race and to do better. The ache persists, but I am experiencing hope. As I walk across the living room to turn the stereo on, music to bake by, my gaze meets that of a bald eagle. He is perched on my balcony rail. What's he doing in New York? He is shockingly similar in appearance to my dead father, an Irish bald eagle.

"I will stop acting sorry for myself," I say aloud to him. He holds my gaze for a few seconds, and then heads off in the direction of the Hudson. "They have really good lox at Zabar's," I shout out after him. I am not sure if he has heard me, but am certain he does not care.

SEPTEMBER 3

"Being safe doesn't make a statement." I read that in a magazine this morning. Obviously my life has been a statement. Of course, the article was referring to the use of fashion accessories, but whatever. Life, the proper silk scarf, it's all the same thing really. Whatever you do you must do with confidence and savoir faire.

I am heading across the park dressed in a vintage black shift. I am not defeated. I am chic and understated. A businesswoman who can get the job done. I am meeting an acquaintance of Barry Hovington's, a Bond Street winner who has hopes of becoming a Hollywood player. He is starting a film company. And I am the perfect person to run it. I walk deliberately to Madison and Seventy-sixth Street and into the Carlyle Hotel.

The lounge area between the bar and the dining room in which I am seated is empty. Am I the last person remaining on the Upper East Side? Is everyone else in St. Tropez? Vacationers be damned. Anyone not in the city is frivolous. They are the money-grubbing upper management of yesterday, so nineties, poor dears. I am here in the city ready to go. I am earnest and hardworking. I imagine myself at the head of a boardroom table dispensing orders with grace. I look at my watch. There is a limit to this self-motivational crap. Where is this Bozo anyway?

"Want to hear my problems?" I ask the middle-aged waiter as he pours more hot water into the proper Carlyle teapot. I am eager for a little harmless chatter, anything to break up the monotony of staring and sipping, sipping and staring. He is having none of it. A vintage New Yorker, he shrugs and moves on.

Two hours and you are definitely a loser. At one hundred eighteen minutes I decide I am throwing in the towel. Just as I am demurely removing the linen napkin from my lap, the most amazing creature appears. To say he looms is an understatement. He is well over six feet. He is completely bald and so large that he lurches forward as he moves, a severed redwood poised to fall.

"Timber," I say under my breath as he attempts to position his rather large ass on the proper upright chaise across the table from me.

"I beg your pardon?" he says in the most upper-crust British accent.

I respond with a slight shrug, careful not to repeat my admonishing "timber."

"I have just come from the bush country in Kenya," he begins. "A lovely black-tie affair, quite a chuckle."

So this is why he is two hours late for tea?

"Have you been to Kenya?" he asks.

"No," I say. "Barry tells me you are starting a film company,"

I continue. I am in no mood for chitchat. That was for two hours ago.

"Ah, yes," he says. "I love films, don't you?" Is he batting his eyelashes?

"As you know, I was Barry's agent until recently," I start in again, an attempt to reel him in.

And then I feel it. His hand is on my knee. I readjust, choosing to believe it is an accident. When you are that large such accidents are probably quite commonplace.

"Are you funded?" I continue. Always interview the employer. He deliberately places his hand back on my knee.

"Certainly," he says in response to my question.

"I see," I respond.

"Fully," he continues, again with the batting lashes.

I assess the situation. Fully funded British banker who wants to start a film company has his hand on my knee. I stand up.

"Thanks for your time, but I am afraid we are not contemplating the same kind of relationship," I say with as much dignity as I can muster.

"I see," says the Looming Brit with an air of boredom. I turn on my heels and march toward the lobby. Maybe it's not me. Maybe everyone else is an asshole.

I decide to head across the street to Zitomer. I will buy some fabulous new hair products, and some aspirin. My head is throbbing. As I head into the revolving door and toward the light, an unfamiliar hand takes hold of my left shoulder.

"Maria?" the unfamiliar voice questions. I turn back around in the direction of the lobby and Charlie Social Register.

"Hi," I say, a little off my game.

"How come you got so skinny?" he asks. "I almost didn't recognize you."

"Not eating?" I reply in the form of a question.

"That's no good," he informs. He subtly glides me back to the middle of the Carlyle lobby away from the flow of entrance traffic. "Could you wait right here for a moment?"

"Alright," I say.

"I have some business to attend to," he continues. "I will be right back."

I stand alone in the middle of the elegant lobby, imagining his "business." She is tall and blonde with tasteful jewelry. She is an older, more refined version of Harris's fantasy woman. I stop myself. Why do I keep doing that?

"Not this joint," I say as Charlie ushers me into Eli Zabar's Madison Avenue sandwich shop. "The sandwiches here are two hundred bucks apiece."

"Do you know the name of this establishment?" Charlie inquires.

"E.A.T.," I say, spelling it out.

"Exactly my point—eat!" shouts Charlie as we are led to a table by the window. "Two vanilla milkshakes to start, please," says Charlie to the host. "Make those doubles," he adds. There is no stopping him. His enthusiasm is contagious.

When the shakes arrive it is clear he is not kidding. I am meant to go up two dress sizes before the end of lunch.

"Delicious," he exclaims as he takes a respite from his shake. The sweet frothy mixture does in fact taste heavenly and although my head still aches I am definitely starting to feel better.

"So," says Charlie as he leans back in his chair, "where is What's-his-name?"

"Harris?" I ask.

He nods.

"Gone," I say as I wipe away at what I am sure is a rather large milkshake mustache.

"Good," Charlie says. "You can do better."

Next, several sandwiches appear on our table.

"Too much," I say.

"We'll pack up what we don't finish," Charlie assures me as he lustily dives in. "You are responsible for two sandwiches." Aye-aye, I think, as I delight in the sheer pleasure of a runny grilled cheese.

"What'd you do, take the day off?" Charlie asks. I squirm in my chair.

"Actually I am sorta looking for a new job?" I try, not really wanting to go into the details.

"What's wrong with the old one?" he asks.

"Well, I was an agent in the film business, but I lost my job," I finally admit. I am in no mood for tap dancing. This guy has been the head of everything; surely he has heard of getting sacked.

"The film business? What were you doing that for?" he inquires. "A lot of phonies in that business." I smile. Nothing wrong with this guy. "Well, sounds as if you've cleaned house pretty well." He smiles back encouragingly.

"I am totally stuffed," I groan as we head out of the restaurant.

"Great," he says. We head out onto a deserted Madison Avenue. It is nearly the end of summer. It is still hot. After only one decent meal the fuzzy overlay that has filtered my view for weeks is dissipating. New York is coming back into focus.

Charlie and I stand on the street awkwardly. He hesitates, and then: "I am staying at the Union Club if you need anything," he says. I look up into his kind weathered face, lined from skiing, sailing, and life. For the first time I see some sadness there.

"Oh, thanks," I say, knowing I will never call. We walk to the next corner. "Thanks for lunch. It was fun." I extend my hand.

"Delightful," he says, rolling each syllable on his tongue. He has a firm handshake. "Where are you off to?" he inquires.

"Home." I smile. "I am going to walk back around the reservoir."

"Have a good walk," he says.

I turn and head toward Fifth Avenue, never looking back, sort of wishing I'd have walked a few more blocks with him, but also feeling relieved that the encounter is over.

I head into the park en route to my apartment. I meander at the periphery of the reservoir. I try to quiet the voice inside me that keeps asking "Now what?" It is clear to me that I cannot go back. No more inappropriate business associates. No more boyfriends who are not sure if they love me. I want a clean life. I am not exactly sure how to get one, but I know I must behave differently. Maybe I attracted assholes because I was one.

"I vow to myself to no longer be an asshole," I say aloud. A preppie-looking man with a tan summer suit and a briefcase moves quickly away.

"Now a snow cone chaser," I say aloud again, not caring in the least if someone hears me. "I can talk to myself, and no one cares!" I shout out with glee.

"A snow cone, please," I say to the vendor with the little cart positioned near the reservoir. I delight in the sweet syrup oozing from the shards of ice, which are burning my lips and tongue.

I walk a little, enjoying the lush beauty of the park, which in a few weeks will look so different with all of its fall foliage. I breathe in New York. I delight in the sheer pleasure of my existence. I find a nearby bench perched on a hill and sit down so I may properly attend to my dripping cone.

"Maria!" I think I hear someone calling my name in the distance. I look up, but see no one. I return to the melting cone. "Maria!" I hear it again, a breathless shout. I turn around and look behind me. Still nothing. I sit back down. And then in the distance I see Charlie. He slows from a run to a rapid walk as he heads up the slight incline toward my bench. He is sweating.

"Charlie?" I question as he sits down right beside me on the bench. His thigh is gently pressing up against my own. He makes no effort to remove it. I hand him the melting snow cone, which he accepts. I watch him awkwardly navigate the syrupy ice with his tongue, and it makes me laugh.

"What?" he asks, demonstrating a little vulnerability. I shrug. "You want to go to a movie or something?" he asks.

"When?" I ask.

"Tonight," he answers.

"I'd rather hit golf balls out into the abyss off Chelsea Piers," I offer.

Charlie leans back and smiles. "That'd be just great," he enthusiastically replies.

"You know, maybe in some ways when you lose your dreams your whole world opens up," I posit as he continues to be a sport and tries to eat the snow cone.

"What are you babbling about?" he asks, smiling. I shrug again. He lobs the tired cone into the bushes and leans back against the rough edges of the park bench. He looks over at me. I bravely return his gaze. There is no sense in pretending.

"What kind of golf clubs do you have?" he asks.

"The best," I respond.

"Of course." He smiles.

ACKNOWLEDGMENTS

The author gratefully acknowledges the following individuals without whom there would be no book: Barry Munger, Sarah Munger, Andrew Smith, Richard Sakai, Henry Jaglom, Ellen Steloff, Robin Lerner, Pam Wick, Lisa Mcgee, Richard Berger, Susie Fitzgerald, Michael Leeson, Buck Henry, Robert Kahn, Fiona Duff Kahn, Jeff Carpenter, Michael Sigman, Marshall Eisen, Jay Stapleton, John Wentworth, Dave Massey, Alex Morris, Megan Lynch, Julie Grau, and Kassie Evashevski.

Deborah Skelly has been a researcher at Paramount Studios, a television and film development and production executive, and an agent at the William Morris Agency. She lives in Los Angeles where she practices law and is at work on her second novel.